Old Greek Stories

James Baldwin

About the Author

James Baldwin

James Arthur Baldwin (August 2, 1924 – December 1, 1987) was an African American novelist, essayist, playwright, poet, and social critic. His essays, as collected in Notes of a Native Son (1955), explore palpable yet unspoken intricacies of racial, sexual, and class distinctions in Western societies, most notably in mid-20th-century America, and their inevitable if unnameable tensions. Some Baldwin essays are book-length, for instance The Fire Next Time (1963), No Name in the Street (1972), and The Devil Finds Work (1976).

Baldwin's novels and plays fictionalize fundamental personal questions and dilemmas amid complex social and psychological pressures thwarting the equitable integration of not only blacks, but also of gay and bisexual men, while depicting some internalized obstacles to such individuals' quests for acceptance. Such dynamics are prominent in Baldwin's second novel, written well before gay equality was widely espoused in America: Giovanni's Room (1956). Baldwin's first novel, Go Tell It on the Mountain, is said to be his best-known work.

Old Greek Stories

JUPITER AND HIS MIGHTY COMPANY.

Personifacation

A long time ago, when the world was much younger than it is now, people told and believed a great many wonderful stories about wonderful things which neither you nor I have ever seen. They often talked about a certain Mighty Being called Jupiter, or Zeus, who was king of the sky and the earth; and they said that he sat most of the time amid the clouds on the top of a very high mountain where he could look down and see everything that was going on in the earth beneath. He liked to ride on the storm-clouds and hurl burning thunderbolts right and left among the trees and rocks; and he was so very, very mighty that when he nodded, the earth quaked, the mountains trembled and smoked, the sky grew black, and the sun hid his face.

Jupiter had two brothers, both of them terrible fellows, but not nearly so great as himself. The name of one of them was Neptune, or Poseidon, and he was the king of the sea. He had a glittering, golden palace far down in the deep sea-caves where the fishes live and the red coral grows; and whenever he was angry the waves would rise mountain high, and the storm-winds would howl fearfully, and the sea would try to break over the land; and men called him the Shaker of the Earth.

4

The other brother of Jupiter was a sad pale-faced being, whose kingdom was underneath the earth, where the sun never shone and where there was darkness and weeping and sorrow all the time. His name was Pluto, or Aidoneus, and his country was called the Lower World, or the Land of Shadows, or Hades. Men said that whenever any one died, Pluto would send his messenger, or Shadow Leader, to carry that one down into his cheerless kingdom; and for that reason they never spoke well of him, but thought of him only as the enemy of life.

A great number of other Mighty Beings lived with Jupiter amid the clouds on the mountain top,-so many that I can name a very few only. There was Venus, the queen of love and beauty, who was fairer by far than any woman that you or I have ever seen. There was Athena, or Minerva, the queen of the air, who gave people wisdom and taught them how to do very many useful things. There was Juno, the queen of earth and sky, who sat at the right hand of Jupiter and gave him all kinds of advice. There was Mars, the great warrior, whose delight was in the din of battle. There was Mercury, the swift messenger, who had wings on his cap and shoes, and who flew from place to place like the summer clouds when they are driven before the wind. There was Vulcan, a skillful blacksmith, who had his forge in a burning mountain and wrought many wonderful things of iron and copper and gold. And besides these, there were many others about whom you will learn by and by, and about whom men told strange and beautiful stories.

They lived in glittering, golden mansions high up among the clouds-so high indeed that the eyes of men could never see them. But they could look down and see what men were doing, and oftentimes they were said to leave their lofty homes and wander unknown across the land or over the sea.

And of all these Mighty Folk, Jupiter was by far the mightiest.

003

THE GOLDEN AGE.

Jupiter and his Mighty Folk had not always dwelt amid the clouds on the mountain top. In times long past, a wonderful family called Titans had lived there and had ruled over all the world. There were twelve of them-six brothers and six sisters-and they said that their father was the Sky and their mother the Earth. They had the form and looks of men and women, but they were much larger and far more beautiful.

The name of the youngest of these Titans was Saturn; and yet he was so very old that men often called him Father Time. He was the king of the Titans, and so, of course, was the king of all the earth besides.

5

*Kinda like the words
with Adam and Eve in the bible*

Imagery

Men were never so happy as they were during Saturn's reign. It was the true Golden Age then. The springtime lasted all the year. The woods and meadows were always full of blossoms, and the music of singing birds was heard every day and every hour. It was summer and autumn, too, at the same time. Apples and figs and oranges always hung ripe from the trees; and there were purple grapes on the vines, and melons and berries of every kind, which the people had but to pick and eat.

Of course nobody had to do any kind of work in that happy time. There was no such thing as sickness or sorrow or old age. Men and women lived for hundreds and hundreds of years and never became gray or wrinkled or lame, but were always handsome and young. They had no need of houses, for there were no cold days nor storms nor anything to make them afraid.

Sounds relaxing

Nobody was poor, for everybody had the same precious things-the sunlight, the pure air, the wholesome water of the springs, the grass for a carpet, the blue sky for a roof, the fruits and flowers of the woods and meadows. So, of course, no one was richer than another, and there was no money, nor any locks or bolts; for everybody was everybody's friend, and no man wanted to get more of anything than his neighbors had.

Kinda creepy

When these happy people had lived long enough they fell asleep, and their bodies were seen no more. They flitted away through the air, and over the mountains, and across the sea, to a flowery land in the distant west. And some men say that, even to this day, they are wandering happily hither and thither about the earth, causing babies to smile in their cradles, easing the burdens of the toilworn and sick, and blessing mankind everywhere.

What a pity it is that this Golden Age should have come to an end! But it was Jupiter and his brothers who brought about the sad change.

It is hard to believe it, but men say that Jupiter was the son of the old Titan king, Saturn, and that he was hardly a year old when he began to plot how he might wage war against his father. As soon as he was grown up, he persuaded his brothers, Neptune and Pluto, and his sisters, Juno, Ceres, and Vesta, to join him; and they vowed that they would drive the Titans from the earth.

Then followed a long and terrible war. But Jupiter had many mighty helpers. A company of one-eyed monsters called Cyclopes were kept busy all the time, forging thunderbolts in the fire of burning mountains. Three other monsters, each with a hundred hands, were called in to throw rocks and trees against the stronghold of the Titans; and Jupiter himself hurled his sharp lightning darts so thick and fast that the woods were set on fire and the water in the rivers boiled with the heat.

6

Of course, good, quiet old Saturn and his brothers and sisters could not hold out always against such foes as these. At the end of ten years they had to give up and beg for peace. They were bound in chains of the hardest rock and thrown into a prison in the Lower Worlds; and the Cyclopes and the hundred-handed monsters were sent there to be their jailers and to keep guard over them forever.

Then men began to grow dissatisfied with their lot. Some wanted to be rich and own all the good things in the world. Some wanted to be kings and rule over the others. Some who were strong wanted to make slaves of those who were weak. Some broke down the fruit trees in the woods, lest others should eat of the fruit. Some, for mere sport, hunted the timid animals which had always been their friends. Some even killed these poor creatures and ate their flesh for food.

At last, instead of everybody being everybody's friend, everybody was everybody's foe.

Interesting

So, in all the world, instead of peace, there was war; instead of plenty, there was starvation; instead of innocence, there was crime; and instead of happiness, there was misery.

Theres always conciences for your actions

And that was the way in which Jupiter made himself so mighty; and that was the way in which the Golden Age came to an end.

004

THE STORY OF PROMETHEUS.

I. HOW FIRE WAS GIVEN TO MEN.

In those old, old times, there lived two brothers who were not like other men, nor yet like those Mighty Ones who lived upon the mountain top. They were the sons of one of those Titans who had fought against Jupiter and been sent in chains to the strong prison-house of the Lower World.

The name of the elder of these brothers was Prometheus, or Forethought; for he was always thinking of the future and making things ready for what might happen to-morrow, or next week, or next year, or it may be in a hundred years to come. The younger was called Epimetheus, or Afterthought; for he was always so busy thinking of yesterday, or last year, or a hundred years ago, that he had no care at all for what might come to pass after a while.

did they make time?

For some cause Jupiter had not sent these brothers to prison with the rest of the

Strange

7

Titans.

Prometheus did not care to live amid the clouds on the mountain top. He was too busy for that. While the Mighty Folk were spending their time in idleness, drinking nectar and eating ambrosia, he was intent upon plans for making the world wiser and better than it had ever been before. *good idea*

He went out amongst men to live with them and help them; for his heart was filled with sadness when he found that they were no longer happy as they had been during the golden days when Saturn was king. Ah, how very poor and wretched they were! He found them living in caves and in holes of the earth, shivering with the cold because there was no fire, dying of starvation, hunted by wild beasts and by one another-the most miserable of all living creatures.

"If they only had fire," said Prometheus to himself, "they could at least warm themselves and cook their food; and after a while they could learn to make tools and build themselves houses. Without fire, they are worse off than the beasts."

Then he went boldly to Jupiter and begged him to give fire to men, that so they might have a little comfort through the long, dreary months of winter.

great

"Not a spark will I give," said Jupiter. "No, indeed! Why, if men had fire they might become strong and wise like ourselves, and after a while they would drive us out of our kingdom. Let them shiver with cold, and let them live like the beasts. It is best for them to be poor and ignorant, that so we Mighty Ones may thrive and be happy."

Prometheus made no answer; but he had set his heart on helping mankind, and he did not give up. He turned away, and left Jupiter and his mighty company forever.

As he was walking by the shore of the sea he found a reed, or, as some say, a tall stalk of fennel, growing; and when he had broken it off he saw that its hollow center was filled with a dry, soft pith which would burn slowly and keep on fire a long time. He took the long stalk in his hands, and started with it towards the dwelling of the sun in the far east.

"Mankind shall have fire in spite of the tyrant who sits on the mountain top," he said.

Imagary

He reached the place of the sun in the early morning just as the glowing, golden orb was rising from the earth and beginning his daily journey through the sky. He touched the end of the long reed to the flames, and the dry pith caught on fire and burned slowly. Then he turned and hastened back to his own land, carrying with him the precious spark hidden in the hollow center of the plant.

8

He called some of the shivering men from their caves and built a fire for them, and showed them how to warm themselves by it and how to build other fires from the coals. Soon there was a cheerful blaze in every rude home in the land, and men and women gathered round it and were warm and happy, and thankful to Prometheus for the wonderful gift which he had brought to them from the sun.

It was not long until they learned to cook their food and so to eat like men instead of like beasts. They began at once to leave off their wild and savage habits; and instead of lurking in the dark places of the world, they came out into the open air and the bright sunlight, and were glad because life had been given to them.

After that, Prometheus taught them, little by little, a thousand things. He showed them how to build houses of wood and stone, and how to tame sheep and cattle and make them useful, and how to plow and sow and reap, and how to protect themselves from the storms of winter and the beasts of the woods. Then he showed them how to dig in the earth for copper and iron, and how to melt the ore, and how to hammer it into shape and fashion from it the tools and weapons which they needed in peace and war; and when he saw how happy the world was becoming he cried out:

"A new Golden Age shall come, brighter and better by far than the old!"

II. HOW DISEASES AND CARES CAME AMONG MEN.

Things might have gone on very happily indeed, and the Golden Age might really have come again, had it not been for Jupiter. But one day, when he chanced to look down upon the earth, he saw the fires burning, and the people living in houses, and the flocks feeding on the hills, and the grain ripening in the fields, and this made him very angry.

"Who has done all this?" he asked.

And some one answered, "Prometheus!"

"What! that young Titan!" he cried. "Well, I will punish him in a way that will make him wish I had shut him up in the prison-house with his kinsfolk. But as for those puny men, let them keep their fire. I will make them ten times more miserable than they were before they had it."

Of course it would be easy enough to deal with Prometheus at any time, and so Jupiter was in no great haste about it. He made up his mind to distress mankind first; and he thought of a plan for doing it in a very strange, roundabout way.

In the first place, he ordered his blacksmith Vulcan, whose forge was in the crater of a burning mountain, to take a lump of clay which he gave him, and mold it into the form of a woman. Vulcan did as he was bidden; and when he had finished the image, he carried it up to Jupiter, who was sitting among the clouds with all the Mighty Folk around him. It was nothing but a mere lifeless body, but the great blacksmith had given it a form more perfect than that of any statue that has ever been made.

10

"Come now!" said Jupiter, "let us all give some goodly gift to this woman;" and he began by giving her life.

Then the others came in their turn, each with a gift for the marvelous creature. One gave her beauty; and another a pleasant voice; and another good manners; and another a kind heart; and another skill in many arts; and, lastly, some one gave her curiosity. Then they called her Pandora, which means the all-gifted, because she had received gifts from them all.

Pandora was so beautiful and so wondrously gifted that no one could help loving her. When the Mighty Folk had admired her for a time, they gave her to Mercury, the light-footed; and he led her down the mountain side to the place where Prometheus and his brother were living and toiling for the good of mankind. He met Epimetheus first, and said to him:

"Epimetheus, here is a beautiful woman, whom Jupiter has sent to you to be your wife."

005

"Epimetheus, here is a beautiful woman.'"

Prometheus had often warned his brother to beware of any gift that Jupiter might send, for he knew that the mighty tyrant could not be trusted; but when Epimetheus saw Pandora, how lovely and wise she was, he forgot all warnings, and took her home to live with him and be his wife.

Pandora was very happy in her new home; and even Prometheus, when he saw her, was pleased with her loveliness. She had brought with her a golden casket, which Jupiter had given her at parting, and which he had told her held many precious things; but wise Athena, the queen of the air, had warned her never, never to open it, nor look at the things inside.

"They must be jewels," she said to herself; and then she thought of how they would add to her beauty if only she could wear them. "Why did Jupiter give them to me if I should never use them, nor so much as look at them?" she asked.

The more she thought about the golden casket, the more curious she was to see what was in it; and every day she took it down from its shelf and felt of the lid, and tried to peer inside of it without opening it.

"Why should I care for what Athena told me?" she said at last. "She is not beautiful, and jewels would be of no use to her. I think that I will look at them, at any rate. Athena will never know. Nobody else will ever know."

Don't Do I ↑↑↑

She opened the lid a very little, just to peep inside. All at once there was a whirring, rustling sound, and before she could shut it down again, out flew ten thousand strange creatures with death-like faces and gaunt and dreadful forms, such as nobody in all the world had ever seen. They fluttered for a little while about the room, and then flew away to find dwelling-places wherever there were homes of men. They were diseases and cares; for up to that time mankind had not had any kind of sickness, nor felt any troubles of mind, nor worried about what the morrow might bring forth.

These creatures flew into every house, and, without any one seeing them, nestled down in the bosoms of men and women and children, and put an end to all their joy; and ever since that day they have been flitting and creeping, unseen and unheard, over all the land, bringing pain and sorrow and death into every household.

If Pandora had not shut down the lid so quickly, things would have gone much worse. But she closed it just in time to keep the last of the evil creatures from getting out. The name of this creature was Foreboding, and although he was almost half out of the casket, Pandora pushed him back and shut the lid so tight that he could never escape. If he had gone out into the world, men would have known from childhood just what troubles were going to come to them every day of their lives, and they would never have had any joy or hope so long as they lived.

And this was the way in which Jupiter sought to make mankind more miserable than they had been before Prometheus had befriended them.

III. HOW THE FRIEND OF MEN WAS PUNISHED.

The next thing that Jupiter did was to punish Prometheus for stealing fire from the sun. He bade two of his servants, whose names were Strength and Force, to seize the bold Titan and carry him to the topmost peak of the Caucasus Mountains. Then he sent the blacksmith Vulcan to bind him with iron chains and fetter him to the rocks so that he could not move hand or foot.

Vulcan did not like to do this, for he was a friend of Prometheus, and yet he did not dare to disobey. And so the great friend of men, who had given them fire and lifted them out of their wretchedness and shown them how to live, was chained to the mountain peak; and there he hung, with the storm-winds whistling always around him, and the pitiless hail beating in his face, and fierce eagles shrieking in his ears and tearing his body with their cruel claws. Yet he bore all his sufferings without a groan, and never would he beg for mercy or say that he was sorry for what he had done.

Year after year, and age after age, Prometheus hung there. Now and then old Helios, the driver of the sun car, would look down upon him and smile; now and then flocks of birds would bring him messages from far-off lands; once the ocean nymphs came and sang wonderful songs in his hearing; and oftentimes men looked up to him with pitying eyes, and cried out against the tyrant who had placed him there.

Then, once upon a time, a white cow passed that way,-a strangely beautiful cow, with large sad eyes and a face that seemed almost human. She stopped and looked up at the cold gray peak and the giant body which was chained there. Prometheus saw her and spoke to her kindly:

"I know who you are," he said. "You are Io who was once a fair and happy maiden in distant Argos; and now, because of the tyrant Jupiter and his jealous queen, you are doomed to wander from land to land in that unhuman form. But do not lose hope. Go on to the southward and then to the west; and after many days you shall come to the great river Nile. There you shall again become a maiden, but fairer and more beautiful than before; and you shall become the wife of the king of that land, and shall give birth to a son, from whom shall spring the hero who will break my chains and set me free. As for me, I bide in patience the day which not even Jupiter can hasten or delay. Farewell!"

Poor Io would have spoken, but she could not. Her sorrowful eyes looked once more at the suffering hero on the peak, and then she turned and began her long and tiresome journey to the land of the Nile.

Ages passed, and at last a great hero whose name was Hercules came to the land

14

of the Caucasus. In spite of Jupiter's dread thunderbolts and fearful storms of snow and sleet, he climbed the rugged mountain peak; he slew the fierce eagles that had so long tormented the helpless prisoner on those craggy heights; and with a mighty blow, he broke the fetters of Prometheus and set the grand old hero free.

"I knew that you would come," said Prometheus. "Ten generations ago I spoke of you to Io, who was afterwards the queen of the land of the Nile."

"And Io," said Hercules, "was the mother of the race from which I am sprung."

006

THE FLOOD.

In those very early times there was a man named Deucalion, and he was the son of Prometheus. He was only a common man and not a Titan like his great father, and yet he was known far and wide for his good deeds and the uprightness of his life. His wife's name was Pyrrha, and she was one of the fairest of the daughters of men.

After Jupiter had bound Prometheus on Mount Caucasus and had sent diseases and cares into the world, men became very, very wicked. They no longer built houses and tended their flocks and lived together in peace; but every man was at war with his neighbor, and there was no law nor safety in all the land. Things were in much worse case now than they had been before Prometheus had come among men, and that was just what Jupiter wanted. But as the world became wickeder and wickeder every day, he began to grow weary of seeing so much bloodshed and of hearing the cries of the oppressed and the poor.

"These men," he said to his mighty company, "are nothing but a source of trouble. When they were good and happy, we felt afraid lest they should become greater than ourselves; and now they are so terribly wicked that we are in worse danger than before. There is only one thing to be done with them, and that is to destroy them every one."

So he sent a great rain-storm upon the earth, and it rained day and night for a long time; and the sea was filled to the brim, and the water ran over the land and covered first the plains and then the forests and then the hills. But men kept on fighting and robbing, even while the rain was pouring down and the sea was coming up over the land.

No one but Deucalion, the son of Prometheus, was ready for such a storm. He had never joined in any of the wrong doings of those around him, and had often told them that unless they left off their evil ways there would be a day of reckoning in the end. Once every year he had gone to the land of the Caucasus to talk with his father, who was hanging chained to the mountain peak.

"The day is coming," said Prometheus, "when Jupiter will send a flood to destroy mankind from the earth. Be sure that you are ready for it, my son."

And so when the rain began to fall, Deucalion drew from its shelter a boat which he had built for just such a time. He called fair Pyrrha, his wife, and the two sat in the boat and were floated safely on the rising waters. Day and night, day and night, I cannot tell how long, the boat drifted hither and thither. The tops of the trees were hidden by the flood, and then the hills and then the mountains; and Deucalion and Pyrrha could see nothing anywhere but water, water, water-and they knew that all the people in the land had been drowned.

After a while the rain stopped falling, and the clouds cleared away, and the blue sky and the golden sun came out overhead. Then the water began to sink very fast and to run off the land towards the sea; and early the very next day the boat was drifted high upon a mountain called Parnassus, and Deucalion and Pyrrha stepped out upon the dry land. After that, it was only a short time until the whole country was laid bare, and the trees shook their leafy branches in the wind, and the fields were carpeted with grass and flowers more beautiful than in the days before the flood.

But Deucalion and Pyrrha were very sad, for they knew that they were the only persons who were left alive in all the land. At last they started to walk down the

16

mountain side towards the plain, wondering what would become of them now, all alone as they were in the wide world. While they were talking and trying to think what they should do, they heard a voice behind them. They turned and saw a noble young prince standing on one of the rocks above them. He was very tall, with blue eyes and yellow hair. There were wings on his shoes and on his cap, and in his hands he bore a staff with golden serpents twined around it. They knew at once that he was Mercury, the swift messenger of the Mighty Ones, and they waited to hear what he would say.

"Is there anything that you wish?" he asked. "Tell me, and you shall have whatever you desire."

"We should like, above all things," said Deucalion, "to see this land full of people once more; for without neighbors and friends, the world is a very lonely place indeed."

"Go on down the mountain," said Mercury, "and as you go, cast the bones of your mother over your shoulders behind you;" and, with these words, he leaped into the air and was seen no more.

17

"What did he mean?" asked Pyrrha.

"Surely I do not know," said Deucalion. "But let us think a moment. Who is our mother, if it is not the Earth, from whom all living things have sprung? And yet what could he mean by the bones of our mother?"

good thinking

"As they walked they picked up the loose stones in their way."

"Perhaps he meant the stones of the earth," said Pyrrha. "Let us go on down the mountain, and as we go, let us pick up the stones in our path and throw them over our shoulders behind us."

"It is rather a silly thing to do," said Deucalion; "and yet there can be no harm in it, and we shall see what will happen."

And so they walked on, down the steep slope of Mount Parnassus, and as they walked they picked up the loose stones in their way and cast them over their shoulders; and strange to say, the stones which Deucalion threw sprang up as full-grown men, strong, and handsome, and brave; and the stones which Pyrrha threw sprang up as full-grown women, lovely and fair. When at last they reached the plain they found themselves at the head of a noble company of human beings, all eager to serve them.

So Deucalion became their king, and he set them in homes, and taught them how to till the ground, and how to do many useful things; and the land was filled with people who were happier and far better than those who had dwelt there before the flood. And they named the country Hellas, after Hellen, the son of Deucalion and Pyrrha; and the people are to this day called Hellenes.

But we call the country GREECE.

008

THE STORY OF IO.

In the town of Argos there lived a maiden named Io. She was so fair and good that all who knew her loved her, and said that there was no one like her in the whole world. When Jupiter, in his home in the clouds, heard of her, he came down to Argos to see her. She pleased him so much, and was so kind and wise, that he came back the next day and the next and the next; and by and by he stayed in Argos all the time so that he might be near her. She did not know who he was, but thought that he was a prince from some far-off land; for he came in the guise of a young man, and did not look like the great king of earth and sky that he was.

But Juno, the queen who lived with Jupiter and shared his throne in the midst of the clouds, did not love Io at all. When she heard why Jupiter stayed from home so long, she made up her mind to do the fair girl all the harm that she could; and one day she went down to Argos to try what could be done.

21

Jupiter saw her while she was yet a great way off, and he knew why she had come. So, to save Io from her, he changed the maiden to a white cow. He thought that when Juno had gone back home, it would not be hard to give Io her own form again.

But when the queen saw the cow, she knew that it was Io.

"Oh, what a fine cow you have there!" she said. "Give her to me, good Jupiter, give her to me!"

Jupiter did not like to do this; but she coaxed so hard that at last he gave up, and let her have the cow for her own. He thought that it would not be long till he could get her away from the queen, and change her to a girl once more. But Juno was too wise to trust him. She took the cow by her horns, and led her out of the town.

"Now, my sweet maid," she said, "I will see that you stay in this shape as long as you live."

Then she gave the cow in charge of a strange watchman named Argus, who had, not two eyes only, as you and I have, but ten times ten. And Argus led the cow to a grove, and tied her by a long rope to a tree, where she had to stand and eat grass, and cry, "Moo! moo!" from morn till night; and when the sun had set, and it was dark, she lay down on the cold ground and wept, and cried, "Moo! moo!" till she fell asleep.

But no kind friend heard her, and no one came to help her; for none but Jupiter and Juno knew that the white cow who stood in the grove was Io, whom all the world loved. Day in and day out, Argus, who was all eyes, sat on a hill close by and kept watch; and you could not say that he went to sleep at all, for while half of his eyes were shut, the other half were wide awake, and thus they slept and watched by turns.

Jupiter was grieved when he saw to what a hard life Io had been doomed, and he tried to think of some plan to set her free. One day he called sly Mercury, who had wings on his shoes, and bade him go and lead the cow away from the grove where she was kept. Mercury went down and stood near the foot of the hill where Argus sat, and began to play sweet tunes on his flute. This was just what the strange watchman liked to hear; and so he called to Mercury, and asked him to come up and sit by his side and play still other tunes.

Mercury did as he wished, and played such strains of sweet music as no one in all the world has heard from that day to this. And as he played, queer old Argus lay down upon the grass and listened, and thought that he had not had so great a treat in all his life. But by and by those sweet sounds wrapped him in so strange a spell that all his eyes closed at once, and he fell into a deep sleep.

This was just what Mercury wished. It was not a brave thing to do, and yet he drew a long, sharp knife from his belt and cut off the head of poor Argus while he slept. Then he ran down the hill to loose the cow and lead her to the town.

But Juno had seen him kill her watchman, and she met him on the road. She cried out to him and told him to let the cow go; and her face was so full of wrath that, as soon as he saw her, he turned and fled, and left poor Io to her fate.

Juno was so much grieved when she saw Argus stretched dead in the grass on the hilltop, that she took his hundred eyes and set them in the tail of a peacock; and there you may still see them to this day.

Then she found a great gadfly, as big as a bat, and sent it to buzz in the white cow's ears, and to bite her and sting her so that she could have no rest all day long. Poor Io ran from place to place to get out of its way; but it buzzed and buzzed, and stung and stung, till she was wild with fright and pain, and wished that she were dead. Day after day she ran, now through the thick woods, now in the long grass that grew on the treeless plains, and now by the shore of the sea.

009

She cried out to him and said "Let the cow go."

By and by she came to a narrow neck of the sea, and, since the land on the other side looked as though she might find rest there, she leaped into the waves and swam across; and that place has been called Bosphorus-a word which means the Sea of the Cow-from that time till now, and you will find it so marked on the maps which you use at school. Then she went on through a strange land on the other side, but, let her do what she would, she could not get rid of the gadfly.

After a time she came to a place where there were high mountains with snow-capped peaks which seemed to touch the sky. There she stopped to rest a while; and she looked up at the calm, cold cliffs above her and wished that she might die where all was so grand and still. But as she looked she saw a giant form stretched upon the rocks midway between earth and sky, and she knew at once that it was Prometheus, the young Titan, whom Jupiter had chained there because he had given fire to men.

"My sufferings are not so great as his," she thought; and her eyes were filled with tears.

Then Prometheus looked down and spoke to her, and his voice was very mild and kind.

"I know who you are," he said; and then he told her not to lose hope, but to go south and then west, and she would by and by find a place in which to rest.

She would have thanked him if she could; but when she tried to speak she could only say, "Moo! moo!"

Then Prometheus went on and told her that the time would come when she should be given her own form again, and that she should live to be the mother of a race of heroes. "As for me," said he, "I bide the time in patience, for I know that one of those heroes will break my chains and set me free. Farewell!"

Then Io, with a brave heart, left the great Titan and journeyed, as he had told her,

25

first south and then west. The gadfly was worse now than before, but she did not fear it half so much, for her heart was full of hope. For a whole year she wandered, and at last she came to the land of Egypt in Africa. She felt so tired now that she could go no farther, and so she lay down near the bank of the great River Nile to rest.

All this time Jupiter might have helped her had he not been so much afraid of Juno. But now it so chanced that when the poor cow lay down by the bank of the Nile, Queen Juno, in her high house in the clouds, also lay down to take a nap. As soon as she was sound asleep, Jupiter like a flash of light sped over the sea to Egypt. He killed the cruel gadfly and threw it into the river. Then he stroked the cow's head with his hand, and the cow was seen no more; but in her place stood the young girl Io, pale and frail, but fair and good as she had been in her old home in the town of Argos. Jupiter said not a word, nor even showed himself to the tired, trembling maiden. He hurried back with all speed to his high home in the clouds, for he feared that Juno might waken and find out what he had done.

The people of Egypt were kind to Io, and gave her a home in their sunny land; and by and by the king of Egypt asked her to be his wife, and made her his queen; and she lived a long and happy life in his marble palace on the bank of the Nile. Ages afterward, the great-grandson of the great-grandson of Io's great-grandson broke the chains of Prometheus and set that mighty friend of mankind free.

The name of the hero was Hercules.

010

0101

THE WONDERFUL WEAVER.

I. THE WARP.

There was a young girl in Greece whose name was Arachne. Her face was pale but fair, and her eyes were big and blue, and her hair was long and like gold. All that she cared to do from morn till noon was to sit in the sun and spin; and all that she cared to do from noon till night was to sit in the shade and weave.

26

And oh, how fine and fair were the things which she wove in her loom! Flax, wool, silk-she worked with them all; and when they came from her hands, the cloth which she had made of them was so thin and soft and bright that men came from all parts of the world to see it. And they said that cloth so rare could not be made of flax, or wool, or silk, but that the warp was of rays of sunlight and the woof was of threads of gold.

Then as, day by day, the girl sat in the sun and span, or sat in the shade and wove, she said: "In all the world there is no yarn so fine as mine, and in all the world there is no cloth so soft and smooth, nor silk so bright and rare."

011

"'Arachne, I am Athena, the Queen of the air.'"

"Who taught you to spin and weave so well?" some one asked.

"No one taught me," she said. "I learned how to do it as I sat in the sun and the shade; but no one showed me."

"But it may be that Athena, the queen of the air, taught you, and you did not know it."

"Athena, the queen of the air? Bah!" said Arachne. "How could she teach me? Can she spin such skeins of yarn as these? Can she weave goods like mine? I should like to see her try. I can teach her a thing or two."

She looked up and saw in the doorway a tall woman wrapped in a long cloak. Her face was fair to see, but stern, oh, so stern! and her gray eyes were so sharp and bright that Arachne could not meet her gaze.

"Arachne," said the woman, "I am Athena, the queen of the air, and I have heard your boast. Do you still mean to say that I have not taught you how to spin and weave?"

"No one has taught me," said Arachne; "and I thank no one for what I know;" and she stood up, straight and proud, by the side of her loom.

"And do you still think that you can spin and weave as well as I?" said Athena.

Arachne's cheeks grew pale, but she said: "Yes. I can weave as well as you."

"Then let me tell you what we will do," said Athena. "Three days from now we will both weave; you on your loom, and I on mine. We will ask all the world to come and see us; and great Jupiter, who sits in the clouds, shall be the judge. And if your work is best, then I will weave no more so long as the world shall last; but if my work is best, then you shall never use loom or spindle or distaff again. Do you agree to this?" "I agree," said Arachne.

28

"It is well," said Athena. And she was gone.

II. THE WOOF.

When the time came for the contest in weaving, all the world was there to see it, and great Jupiter sat among the clouds and looked on.

Arachne had set up her loom in the shade of a mulberry tree, where butterflies were flitting and grasshoppers chirping all through the livelong day. But Athena had set up her loom in the sky, where the breezes were blowing and the summer sun was shining; for she was the queen of the air.

Then Arachne took her skeins of finest silk and began to weave. And she wove a web of marvelous beauty, so thin and light that it would float in the air, and yet so strong that it could hold a lion in its meshes; and the threads of warp and woof were of many colors, so beautifully arranged and mingled one with another that all who saw were filled with delight.

"No wonder that the maiden boasted of her skill," said the people.

And Jupiter himself nodded.

Then Athena began to weave. And she took of the sunbeams that gilded the mountain top, and of the snowy fleece of the summer clouds, and of the blue ether of the summer sky, and of the bright green of the summer fields, and of the royal purple of the autumn woods,-and what do you suppose she wove?

The web which she wove in the sky was full of enchanting pictures of flowers and gardens, and of castles and towers, and of mountain heights, and of men and beasts, and of giants and dwarfs, and of the mighty beings who dwell in the clouds with Jupiter. And those who looked upon it were so filled with wonder and delight, that they forgot all about the beautiful web which Arachne had woven. And Arachne herself was ashamed and afraid when she saw it; and she hid her face in her hands and wept.

"Oh, how can I live," she cried, "now that I must never again use loom or spindle or distaff?"

And she kept on, weeping and weeping and weeping, and saying, "How can I live?"

Then, when Athena saw that the poor maiden would never have any joy unless she were allowed to spin and weave, she took pity on her and said:

"I would free you from your bargain if I could, but that is a thing which no one can do. You must hold to your agreement never to touch loom or spindle again. And yet, since you will never be happy unless you can spin and weave, I will give you a new form so that you can carry on your work with neither spindle nor loom."

Then she touched Arachne with the tip of the spear which she sometimes carried; and the maiden was changed at once into a nimble spider, which ran into a shady place in the grass and began merrily to spin and weave a beautiful web.

I have heard it said that all the spiders which have been in the world since then are the children of Arachne; but I doubt whether this be true. Yet, for aught I know, Arachne still lives and spins and weaves; and the very next spider that you see may be she herself.

012

THE LORD OF THE SILVER BOW.

I. DELOS.

Long before you or I or anybody else can remember, there lived with the Mighty Folk on the mountain top a fair and gentle lady named Leto. So fair and gentle was she that Jupiter loved her and made her his wife. But when Juno, the queen of earth and sky, heard of this, she was very angry; and she drove Leto down from the mountain and bade all things great and small refuse to help her. So Leto fled like a wild deer from land to land and could find no place in which to rest. She could not stop, for then the ground would quake under her feet, and the stones would cry out, "Go on! go on!" and birds and beasts and trees and men would join in the cry; and no one in all the wide land took pity on her.

One day she came to the sea, and as she fled along the beach she lifted up her hands and called aloud to great Neptune to help her. Neptune, the king of the sea, heard her and was kind to her. He sent a huge fish, called a dolphin, to bear her away from the cruel land; and the fish, with Leto sitting on his broad back, swam through the waves to Delos, a little island which lay floating on top of the water like a boat. There the gentle lady found rest and a home; for the place belonged to Neptune, and the words of cruel Juno were not obeyed there. Neptune put four marble pillars under the island so that it should rest firm upon them; and then he chained it fast, with great chains which reached to the bottom of the sea, so that the waves might never move it.

By and by twin babes were born to Leto in Delos. One was a boy whom she called Apollo, the other a girl whom she named Artemis, or Diana. When the news of

30

their birth was carried to Jupiter and the Mighty Folk on the mountain top, all the world was glad. The sun danced on the waters, and singing swans flew seven times round the island of Delos. The moon stooped to kiss the babes in their cradle; and Juno forgot her anger, and bade all things on the earth and in the sky be kind to Leto.

The two children grew very fast. Apollo became tall and strong and graceful; his face was as bright as the sunbeams; and he carried joy and gladness with him wherever he went. Jupiter gave him a pair of swans and a golden chariot, which bore him over sea and land wherever he wanted to go; and he gave him a lyre on which he played the sweetest music that was ever heard, and a silver bow with sharp arrows which never missed the mark. When Apollo went out into the world, and men came to know about him, he was called by some the Bringer of Light, by others the Master of Song, and by still others the Lord of the Silver Bow.

Diana was tall and graceful, too, and very handsome. She liked to wander in the woods with her maids, who were called nymphs; she took kind care of the timid deer and the helpless creatures which live among the trees; and she delighted in hunting wolves and bears and other savage beasts. She was loved and feared in every land, and Jupiter made her the queen of the green woods and the chase.

II. DELPHI.

"Where is the center of the world?"

This is the question which some one asked Jupiter as he sat in his golden hall. Of course the mighty ruler of earth and sky was too wise to be puzzled by so simple a thing, but he was too busy to answer it at once. So he said:

"Come again in one year from to-day, and I will show you the very place."

Then Jupiter took two swift eagles which could fly faster than the storm-wind, and trained them till the speed of the one was the same as that of the other. At the end of the year he said to his servants:

"Take this eagle to the eastern rim of the earth, where the sun rises out of the sea; and carry his fellow to the far west, where the ocean is lost in darkness and nothing lies beyond. Then, when I give you the sign, loosen both at the same moment."

The servants did as they were bidden, and carried the eagles to the outermost edges of the world. Then Jupiter clapped his hands. The lightning flashed, the thunder rolled, and the two swift birds were set free. One of them flew straight back towards the west, the other flew straight back towards the east; and no arrow ever sped faster from the bow than did these two birds from the hands of those who had held them.

On and on they went like shooting stars rushing to meet each other; and Jupiter and all his mighty company sat amid the clouds and watched their flight. Nearer and nearer they came, but they swerved not to the right nor to the left. Nearer and nearer-and then with a crash like the meeting of two ships at sea, the eagles came together in mid-air and fell dead to the ground.

"Who asked where is the center of the world?" said Jupiter. "The spot where the two eagles lie-that is the center of the world."

They had fallen on the top of a mountain in Greece which men have ever since called Parnassus.

"If that is the center of the world," said young Apollo, "then I will make my home there, and I will build a house in that place, so that my light may be seen in all lands."

So Apollo went down to Parnassus, and looked about for a spot in which to lay the foundations of his house. The mountain itself was savage and wild, and the valley below it was lonely and dark. The few people who lived there kept themselves hidden among the rocks as if in dread of some great danger. They told Apollo that near the foot of the mountain where the steep cliff seemed to be split in two there lived a huge serpent called the Python. This serpent often seized sheep and cattle, and sometimes even men and women and children, and carried them up to his dreadful den and devoured them.

"Can no one kill this beast?" said Apollo.

And they said, "No one; and we and our children and our flocks shall all be slain by him."

Then Apollo with his silver bow in his hands went up towards the place where the Python lay. The monster had worn great paths through the grass and among the rocks, and his lair was not hard to find. When he caught sight of Apollo, he uncoiled himself, and came out to meet him. The bright prince saw the creature's glaring eyes and blood-red mouth, and heard the rush of his scaly body over the stones. He fitted an arrow to his bow, and stood still. The Python saw that his foe was no common man, and turned to flee. Then the arrow sped from the bow-and the monster was dead.

"Here I will build my house," said Apollo.

Close to the foot of the steep cliff, and beneath the spot where Jupiter's eagles had fallen, he laid the foundations; and soon where had been the lair of the Python, the white walls of Apollo's temple arose among the rocks. Then the poor people of the land came and built their houses near by; and Apollo lived among them many years, and taught them to be gentle and wise, and showed them how to be happy. The mountain was no longer savage and wild, but was a place of music and song; the valley was no longer dark and lonely, but was filled with beauty and light.

"What shall we call our city?" the people asked.

"Call it Delphi, or the Dolphin," said Apollo; "for it was a dolphin that carried my mother across the sea."

III. DAPHNE.

In the Vale of Tempe, which lies far north of Delphi, there lived a young girl whose name was Daphne. She was a strange child, wild and shy as a fawn, and as fleet of foot as the deer that feed on the plains. But she was as fair and good as a day in June, and none could know her but to love her.

Daphne spent the most of her time in the fields and woods, with the birds and blossoms and trees; and she liked best of all to wander along the banks of the River Peneus, and listen to the ripple of the water as it flowed among the reeds or over the shining pebbles. Very often she would sing and talk to the river as if it were a living thing, and could hear her; and she fancied that it understood what she said, and that it whispered many a wonderful secret to her in return. The good people who knew her best said:

"She is the child of the river."

34

"Yes, dear river," she said, "let me be your child."

The river smiled and answered her in a way which she alone could understand; and always, after that, she called it "Father Peneus."

One day when the sun shone warm, and the air was filled with the perfume of flowers, Daphne wandered farther away from the river than she had ever gone before. She passed through a shady wood and climbed a hill, from the top of which she could see Father Peneus lying white and clear and smiling in the valley below. Beyond her were other hills, and then the green slopes and wooded top of great Mount Ossa. Ah, if she could only climb to the summit of Ossa, she might have a view of the sea, and of other mountains close by, and of the twin peaks of Mount Parnassus, far, far to the south!

"Good-by, Father Peneus," she said. "I am going to climb the mountain; but I will come back soon."

The river smiled, and Daphne ran onward, climbing one hill after another, and wondering why the great mountain seemed still so far away. By and by she came to the foot of a wooded slope where there was a pretty waterfall and the ground was bespangled with thousands of beautiful flowers; and she sat down there a moment to rest. Then from the grove on the hilltop above her, came the sound of the loveliest music she had ever heard. She stood up and listened. Some one was playing on a lyre, and some one was singing. She was frightened; and still the music was so charming that she could not run away.

Then, all at once, the sound ceased, and a young man, tall and fair and with a face as bright as the morning sun, came down the hillside towards her.

"Daphne!" he said; but she did not stop to hear. She turned and fled like a frightened deer, back towards the Vale of Tempe.

"Daphne!" cried the young man. She did not know that it was Apollo, the Lord of the Silver Bow; she only knew that the stranger was following her, and she ran as fast as her fleet feet could carry her. No young man had ever spoken to her before, and the sound of his voice filled her heart with fear.

"She is the fairest maiden that I ever saw," said Apollo to himself. "If I could only look at her face again and speak with her, how happy I should be."

Through brake, through brier, over rocks and the trunks of fallen trees, down rugged slopes, across mountain streams, leaping, flying, panting, Daphne ran. She looked not once behind her, but she heard the swift footsteps of Apollo coming always nearer; she heard the rattle of the silver bow which hung from his shoulders; she heard his very breath, he was so close to her. At last she was in the valley where the ground was smooth and it was easier running, but her strength was fast leaving her. Right before her, however, lay the river, white and smiling in the sunlight. She stretched out her arms and cried:

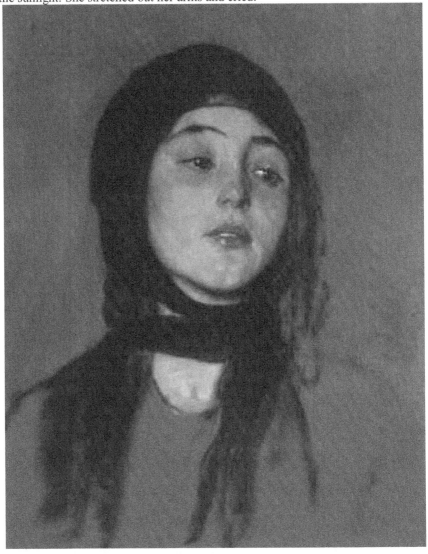

"O Father Peneus, save me!"

013

SHE TURNED AND FLED LIKE A FRIGHTENED DEER.

Personification

Then it seemed as though the river rose up to meet her. The air was filled with a blinding mist. For a moment Apollo lost sight of the fleeing maiden. Then he saw her close by the river's bank, and so near to him that her long hair, streaming behind her, brushed his cheek. He thought that she was about to leap into the rushing, roaring waters, and he reached out his hands to save her. But it was not the fair, timid Daphne that he caught in his arms; it was the trunk of a laurel tree, its green leaves trembling in the breeze.

"O Daphne! Daphne!" he cried, "is this the way in which the river saves you? Does Father Peneus turn you into a tree to keep you from me?"

Whether Daphne had really been turned into a tree, I know not; nor does it matter now-it was so long ago. But Apollo believed that it was so, and hence he made a wreath of the laurel leaves and set it on his head like a crown, and said that he would wear it always in memory of the lovely maiden. And ever after that, the laurel was Apollo's favorite tree, and, even to this day, poets and musicians are crowned with its leaves.

IV. DELUDED.

Apollo did not care to live much of the time with his mighty kinsfolk on the mountain top. He liked better to go about from place to place and from land to land, seeing people at their work and making their lives happy. When men first saw his fair boyish face and his soft white hands, they sneered and said he was only an idle, good-for-nothing fellow. But when they heard him speak, they were so charmed that they stood, spellbound, to listen; and ever after that they made his words their law. They wondered how it was that he was so wise; for it seemed to them that he did nothing but stroll about, playing on his wonderful lyre and looking at the trees and blossoms and birds and bees. But when any of them were sick they came to him, and he told them what to find in plants or stones or brooks that would heal them and make them strong again. They noticed that he did not grow old, as others did, but that he was always young and fair; and, even after he had gone away,-they knew not how, nor whither,-it seemed as though the earth were a brighter and sweeter place to live in than it had been before his coming.

In a mountain village beyond the Vale of Tempe, there lived a beautiful lady named Coronis. When Apollo saw her, he loved her and made her his wife; and for a long time the two lived together, and were happy. By and by a babe was born to them,-a boy with the most wonderful eyes that anybody ever saw,-and they named him AEsculapius. Then the mountains and the woods were filled with the music of Apollo's lyre, and even the Mighty Folk on the mountain top were glad.

One day Apollo left Coronis and her child, and went on a journey to visit his

37

favorite home on Mount Parnassus.

"I shall hear from you every day," he said at parting. "The crow will fly swiftly every morning to Parnassus, and tell me whether you and the child are well, and what you are doing while I am away."

For Apollo had a pet crow which was very wise, and could talk. The bird was not black, like the crows which you have seen, but as white as snow. Men say that all crows were white until that time, but I doubt whether anybody knows.

Apollo's crow was a great tattler, and did not always tell the truth. It would see the beginning of something, and then, without waiting to know anything more about it, would hurry off and make up a great story about it. But there was no one else to carry news from Coronis to Apollo; for, as you know, there were no postmen in those days, and there was not a telegraph wire in the whole world.

All went well for several days. Every morning the white bird would wing its way over hills and plains and rivers and forests until it found Apollo, either in the groves on the top of Parnassus or in his own house at Delphi. Then it would alight upon his shoulder and say, "Coronis is well! Coronis is well!"

One day, however, it had a different story. It came much earlier than ever before, and seemed to be in great haste.

"Cor-Cor-Cor!" it cried; but it was so out of breath that it could not speak her whole name.

"What is the matter?" cried Apollo, in alarm. "Has anything happened to Coronis? Speak! Tell me the truth!"

"She does not love you! she does not love you!" cried the crow. "I saw a man-I saw a man,-" and then, without stopping to take breath, or to finish the story, it flew up into the air, and hurried homeward again.

Apollo, who had always been so wise, was now almost as foolish as his crow. He fancied that Coronis had really deserted him for another man, and his mind was filled with grief and rage. With his silver bow in his hands he started at once for his home. He did not stop to speak with any one; he had made up his mind to learn the truth for himself. His swan-team and his golden chariot were not at hand-for, now that he was living with men, he must travel like men. The journey had to be made on foot, and it was no short journey in those days when there were no roads. But after a time, he came to the village where he had lived happily for so many years, and soon he saw his own house half-hidden among the dark-leaved olive trees. In another minute he would know whether the crow had told him the truth.

38

He heard the footsteps of some one running in the grove. He caught a glimpse of a white robe among the trees. He felt sure that this was the man whom the crow had seen, and that he was trying to run away. He fitted an arrow to his bow quickly. He drew the string. Twang! And the arrow which never missed sped like a flash of light through the air.

Apollo heard a sharp, wild cry of pain; and he bounded forward through the grove. There, stretched dying on the grass, he saw his dear Coronis. She had seen him coming, and was running gladly to greet him, when the cruel arrow pierced her heart. Apollo was overcome with grief. He took her form in his arms, and tried to call her back to life again. But it was all in vain. She could only whisper his name, and then she was dead.

A moment afterwards the crow alighted on one of the trees near by. "Cor-Cor-Cor," it began; for it wanted now to finish its story. But Apollo bade it begone.

"Cursed bird," he cried, "you shall never say a word but 'Cor-Cor-Cor!' all your life; and the feathers of which you are so proud shall no longer be white, but black as midnight."

And from that time to this, as you very well know, all crows have been black; and they fly from one dead tree to another, always crying, "Cor-cor-cor!"

V. DISGRACED.

Soon after this, Apollo took the little AEsculapius in his arms and carried him to a wise old schoolmaster named Cheiron, who lived in a cave under the gray cliffs of a mountain close by the sea.

"Take this child," he said, "and teach him all the lore of the mountains, the woods, and the fields. Teach him those things which he most needs to know in order to do great good to his fellow-men."

And AEsculapius proved to be a wise child, gentle and sweet and teachable; and among all the pupils of Cheiron he was the best loved. He learned the lore of the mountains, the woods, and the fields. He found out what virtue there is in herbs and flowers and senseless stones; and he studied the habits of birds and beasts and men. But above all he became skillful in dressing wounds and healing diseases; and to this day physicians remember and honor him as the first and greatest of their craft. When he grew up to manhood his name was heard in every land, and people blessed him because he was the friend of life and the foe of death.

As time went by, AEsculapius cured so many people and saved so many lives that Pluto, the pale-faced king of the Lower World, became alarmed.

"I shall soon have nothing to do," he said, "if this physician does not stop keeping people away from my kingdom."

And he sent word to his brother Jupiter, and complained that AEsculapius was cheating him out of what was his due. Great Jupiter listened to his complaint, and stood up among the storm clouds, and hurled his thunderbolts at AEsculapius until the great physician was cruelly slain. Then all the world was filled with grief, and even the beasts and the trees and the stones wept because the friend of life was no more.

When Apollo heard of the death of his son, his grief and wrath were terrible. He could not do anything against Jupiter and Pluto, for they were stronger than he; but he went down into the smithy of Vulcan, underneath the smoking mountains, and slew the giant smiths who had made the deadly thunderbolts.

Then Jupiter, in his turn, was angry, and ordered Apollo to come before him and be punished for what he had done. He took away his bow and arrows and his wonderful lyre and all his beauty of form and feature; and after that Jupiter clothed him in the rags of a beggar and drove him down from the mountain, and told him that he should never come back nor be himself again until he had served some man a whole year as a slave.

And so Apollo went out, alone and friendless, into the world; and no one who saw him would have dreamed that he was once the sun-bright Lord of the Silver Bow.

014

015

ADMETUS AND ALCESTIS.

I. THE SLAVE.

In a little town north of Delphi, and not very far from the sea, there lived a young man named Admetus. He was the ruler of the town, and hence was called its king; but his kingdom was so small that he could walk all round it in half a day. He knew the name of every man and woman and child in the town, and everybody loved him because he was so gentle and kind and at the same time a king.

Late one day, when the rain was falling and the wind was blowing cold from the mountains, a beggar came to his door. The man was ragged and dirty and half starved, and Admetus knew that he must have come from some strange land, for in his own country no one ever went hungry. So the kind king took him into the house and fed him; and after the man had bathed he gave him his own warm cloak, and bade the servants make a place for him to sleep through the night.

In the morning Admetus asked the poor man his name, but he shook his head and made no answer. Then Admetus asked him about his home and his country; and all that the man would say was: "Make me your slave, master! Make me your slave, and let me serve you for a year."

The young king did not need another servant. But he saw that the poorest slave in the land was better off than this man, and so he took pity on him. "I will do as you ask," he said. "I will give you a home and food and clothing; and you shall serve me and be my slave for one year."

There was but little that the stranger knew how to do, and so he was sent to the hills to take care of the king's sheep and goats. For a whole year he tended the flocks, finding the greenest pastures and the freshest water for them, and keeping the wolves away. Admetus was very kind to him, as he was to all his servants, and the food and clothing which he gave him were of the best in the land. But the stranger did not tell his name nor say anything about his kindred or his home.

When a year and a day had passed, it so happened that Admetus was walking out among the hills to see his sheep. All at once the sound of music fell upon his ear. It was no such music as shepherds play, but sweeter and richer than any he had ever heard before. He looked to see where the sound came from. Ah! who was that sitting on the hilltop, with the sheep around him listening to his music? Surely it was not his shepherd?

It was a tall and handsome young man, clad in robes lighter and finer than any king might wear. His face was as bright as sunbeams, and his eyes gleamed like lightning. Upon his shoulder was a silver bow, from his belt hung a quiver of sharp arrows, and in his hands was a golden lyre. Admetus stood still and wondered. Then the stranger spoke:

"King Admetus," he said, "I am the poor beggar whom you fed-your slave to whom you were so kind. I have served you, as I agreed, for a whole year, and now I am going home. Is there anything I can do for you?"

"Yes," said Admetus; "tell me your name."

"My name is Apollo," was the answer. "Twelve months ago my father, mighty Jupiter, drove me away from before his face and bade me go out friendless and alone upon the earth; and he told me that I should not turn again towards home until I had served a year as some man's slave. I came to you, ragged and half starved, and you fed and clothed me; and I became your slave, and you were as kind to me as though I were your son. What shall I give you to reward you?"

"Lord of the Silver Bow," said the king, "I have all that any man can want. I am happy in the thought that I have been of some help to you. I can ask for nothing more."

"Very well," said Apollo; "but if the time should ever come when you need my help, let me know."

Then the bright prince walked swiftly away, playing sweet music as he went; and Admetus with glad heart returned to his home.

II. THE CHARIOT.

From the place where Admetus lived it was only a few miles to Iolcus, a rich city by the sea. The king of Iolcus was a cruel tyrant named Pelias, who cared for nobody in all the world but himself. This Pelias had a daughter named Alcestis, who was as fair as any rose in June and so gentle and good that everybody praised her. Many a prince from over the sea had come to woo Alcestis for his wife; and the noblest young men in Greece had tried to win her favor. But there was only

42

one to whom she would listen, and that was her young neighbor, King Admetus.

So Admetus went before gruff King Pelias to ask him whether he might wed Alcestis.

"No one shall have my daughter," said the old king, "until he proves that he is worthy to be my son-in-law. If you want her, you must come for her in a chariot drawn by a lion and a wild boar. If you come in any other way, she shall not be your wife." And Pelias laughed, and drove the young man out of his palace.

[handwritten in margin: this dadis crazy]

Admetus went away feeling very sad; for who had ever heard of harnessing a lion and a wild boar together in a chariot? The bravest man in the world could not do such a thing as that.

As he walked along and saw the sheep and goats feeding on the hilltops near his own town, he chanced to think of Apollo and of the last words that he had heard him say: "When you need my help, let me know."

"I will let him know," said Admetus.

Early the next morning he built an altar of stones in the open field; and when he had killed the fattest goat of the flock, he built a fire on the altar and laid the thighs of the goat in the flames. Then when the smell of the burning flesh went up into the air, he lifted his hands towards the mountain tops and called to Apollo.

"Lord of the Silver Bow," he cried, "if ever I have shown kindness to the poor and the distressed, come now and help me. For I am in sore need, and I remember your promise."

Hardly was he done speaking when bright Apollo, bearing his bow and his quiver of arrows, came down and stood before him.

"Kindest of kings," he said, "tell me how I can help you."

Then Admetus told him all about the fair Alcestis, and how her father would give her only to the man who should come for her in a chariot drawn by a lion and a wild boar.

"Come with me," said Apollo, "and I will help you."

Then the two went together into the forest, the Lord of the Silver Bow leading the way. Soon they started a lion from its lair and gave chase to it. The fleet-footed Apollo seized the beast by its mane, and although it howled and snapped with its fierce jaws it did not touch him. Then Admetus started a wild boar from a thicket. Apollo gave chase to it, too, making the lion run beside him like a dog. When he

[handwritten in margin: metiphor]

43

had caught the boar, he went on through the forest, leading the two beasts, one with his right hand, the other with his left; and Admetus followed behind.

IT WAS A STRANGE TEAM

It was not yet noon when they came to the edge of the woods and saw the sea and the city of Iolcus only a little way off. A golden chariot stood by the roadside as if waiting for them, and the lion and the boar were soon harnessed to it. It was a strange team, and the two beasts tried hard to fight each other; but Apollo lashed them with a whip and tamed them until they lost their fierceness and were ready to mind the rein. Then Admetus climbed into the chariot; and Apollo stood by his side and held the reins and the whip, and drove into Iolcus.

Old King Pelias was astonished when he saw the wonderful chariot and the glorious charioteer; and when Admetus again asked him for the fair Alcestis, he could not refuse. A day was set for the wedding, and Apollo drove his team back to the forest and set the lion and the wild boar free.

And so Admetus and Alcestis were married, and everybody in the two towns, except gruff old King Pelias, was glad. Apollo himself was one of the guests at the wedding feast, and he brought a present for the young bridegroom; it was a promise from the Mighty Folk upon the mountain top that if Admetus should ever be sick and in danger of death, he might become well again if some one who loved him would die for him.

III. THE SHADOW LEADER.

Admetus and Alcestis lived together happily for a long time, and all the people in their little kingdom loved and blessed them. But at last Admetus fell sick, and, as he grew worse and worse every day, all hope that he would ever get well was lost. Then those who loved him remembered the wedding gift which Apollo had given him, and they began to ask who would be willing to die in his stead.

His father and mother were very old and could hope to live but a short time at best, and so it was thought that one of them would be glad to give up life for the sake of their son. But when some one asked them about it, they shook their heads and said that though life was short they would cling to it as long as they could.

Then his brothers and sisters were asked if they would die for Admetus, but they loved themselves better than their brother, and turned away and left him. There were men in the town whom he had befriended and who owed their lives to him; they would have done everything else for him, but this thing they would not do.

44

Now while all were shaking their heads and saying "Not I," the beautiful Alcestis went into her own room and called to Apollo and asked that she might give up her life to save her husband. Then without a thought of fear she lay down upon her bed and closed her eyes; and a little while afterward, when her maidens came into the room they found her dead.

At the very same time Admetus felt his sickness leave him, and he sprang up as well and strong as he had ever been. Wondering how it was that he had been so quickly cured, he made haste to find Alcestis and tell her the good news. But when he went into her room, he saw her lying lifeless on her couch, and he knew at once that she had died for him. His grief was so great that he could not speak, and he wished that death had taken him and spared the one whom he loved.

In all the land every eye was wet with weeping for Alcestis, and the cries of the mourners were heard in every house. Admetus sat by the couch where his young queen lay, and held her cold hand in his own. The day passed, and night came, but he would not leave her. All through the dark hours he sat there alone. The morning dawned, but he did not want to see the light.

At last the sun began to rise in the east, and then Admetus was surprised to feel the hand which he held growing warm. He saw a red tinge coming into the pale cheeks of Alcestis.

A moment later the fair lady opened her eyes and sat up, alive and well and glad.

How was it that Alcestis had been given back to life?

When she died and left her body, the Shadow Leader, who knows no pity, led her, as he led all others, to the cheerless halls of Proserpine, the queen of the Lower World.

"Who is this who comes so willingly?" asked the pale-faced queen.

And when she was told how Alcestis, so young and beautiful, had given her life to save that of her husband, she was moved with pity; and she bade the Shadow Leader take her back again to the joy and sunlight of the Upper World.

So it was that Alcestis came to life; and for many years she and Admetus lived in their little kingdom not far from the sea; and the Mighty Ones on the mountain top blessed them; and, at last, when they had become very old, the Shadow Leader led them both away together.

0169

017

CADMUS AND EUROPA.

46

I. THE BULL.

In Asia there lived a king who had two children, a boy and a girl. The boy's name was Cadmus, and the girl's name was Europa. The king's country was a very small one. He could stand on his house top and see the whole of it. On one side of it there were mountains, and on the other side was the sea. The king thought that it was the center of the world, and he did not know much about other lands and people.

Yet he was very happy in his own little kingdom, and very fond of his children. And he had good reason to be proud of them; for Cadmus grew up to be the bravest young man in the land, and Europa to be the fairest maiden that had ever been seen. But sad days came to them all at last.

One morning Europa went out into a field near the seashore to pick flowers. Her father's cattle were in the field, grazing among the sweet clover. They were all very tame, and Europa knew every one of them by name. The herdsman was lying in the shade under a tree, trying to make music on a little flute of straw. Europa had played in the field a thousand times before, and no one had ever thought of any harm befalling her.

That morning she noticed that there was a strange bull with the herd. He was very large and as white as snow; and he had soft brown eyes which somehow made him look very gentle and kind. At first he did not even look at Europa, but went here and there, eating the tender grass which grew among the clover. But when she had gathered her apron full of daisies and buttercups, he came slowly towards her. She was not at all afraid of him; and so she stopped to look at him, he was so handsome. He came close to her, and rubbed her arm with his nose to say "Good-morning!"

She stroked his head and neck, and he seemed much pleased. Then she made a wreath of daisies, and hung it round his neck. He looked at her with his soft kind eyes, and seemed to thank her; and in a little while, he lay down among the clover. Europa then made a smaller wreath, and climbed upon his back to twine it round his horns. But all at once he sprang up, and ran away so swiftly that Europa could not help herself. She did not dare to jump off while he was going so fast, and all that she could think to do was to hold fast to his neck and scream very loud.

The herdsman under the tree heard her scream, and jumped up to see what was the matter. He saw the bull running with her towards the shore. He ran after them as fast as he could, but it was of no use. The bull leaped into the sea, and swam swiftly away, with poor Europa on his back. Several other people had seen him, and now they ran to tell the king. Soon the whole town was alarmed. Everybody ran out to the shore and looked. All that could be seen was something white moving very fast over the calm, blue water; and soon it was out of sight.

The king sent out his fastest ship to try to overtake the bull. The sailors rowed far out to sea, much farther than any ship had ever gone before; but no trace of Europa could be found. When they came back, everybody felt that there was no more hope. All the women and children in the town wept for the lost Europa. The king shut himself up in his house, and did not eat nor drink for three days. Then he called his son Cadmus, and bade him take a ship and go in search of his sister; and he told him that, no matter what dangers might be in his way, he must not come back until she was found.

Cadmus was glad to go. He chose twenty brave young men to go with him, and set sail the very next day. It was a great undertaking; for they were to pass through an unknown sea, and they did not know what lands they would come to. Indeed, it was feared that they would never come to any land at all. Ships did not dare to go far from the shore in those days. But Cadmus and his friends were not afraid. They were ready to face any danger.

In a few days they came to a large island called Cyprus. Cadmus went on shore, and tried to talk with the strange people who lived there. They were very kind to him, but they did not understand his language. At last he made out by signs to tell them who he was, and to ask them if they had seen his little sister Europa or the white bull that had carried her away. They shook their heads and pointed to the west.

Then the young men sailed on in their little ship. They came to many islands, and stopped at every one, to see if they could find any trace of Europa; but they heard no news of her at all. At last, they came to the country which we now call Greece. It was a new country then, and only a few people lived there, and Cadmus soon learned to speak their language well. For a long time he wandered from one little town to another, always telling the story of his lost sister.

II. THE PYTHIA.

One day an old man told Cadmus that if he would go to Delphi and ask the Pythia, perhaps she could tell him all about Europa. Cadmus had never heard of Delphi or of the Pythia, and he asked the old man what he meant.

"I will tell you," said the man. "Delphi is a town, built near the foot of Mount Parnassus, at the very center of the earth. It is the town of Apollo, the Bringer of Light; and there is a temple there, built close to the spot where Apollo killed a black serpent, many, many years ago. The temple is the most wonderful place in the world. In the middle of the floor there is a wide crack, or crevice; and this crevice goes down, down into the rock, nobody knows how deep. A strange odor comes up out of the crevice; and if any one breathes much of it, he is apt to fall

48

over and lose his senses."

"But who is the Pythia that you spoke about?" asked Cadmus.

"I will tell you," said the old man. "The Pythia is a wise woman, who lives in the temple. When anybody asks her a hard question, she takes a three-legged stool, called a tripod, and sets it over the crevice in the floor. Then she sits on the stool and breathes the strange odor; and instead of losing her senses as other people would do, she talks with Apollo; and Apollo tells her how to answer the question. Men from all parts of the world go there to ask about things which they would like to know. The temple is full of the beautiful and costly gifts which they have brought for the Pythia. Sometimes she answers them plainly, and sometimes she answers them in riddles; but what she says always comes true."

So Cadmus went to Delphi to ask the Pythia about his lost sister. The wise woman was very kind to him; and when he had given her a beautiful golden cup to pay her for her trouble, she sat down on the tripod and breathed the strange odor which came up through the crevice in the rock. Then her face grew pale, and her eyes looked wild, and she seemed to be in great pain; but they said that she was talking with Apollo. Cadmus asked her to tell him what had become of Europa. She said that Jupiter, in the form of a white bull, had carried her away, and that it would be of no use to look for her any more.

"But what shall I do?" said Cadmus. "My father told me not to turn back till I should find her."

"Your father is dead," said the Pythia, "and a strange king rules in his place. You must stay in Greece, for there is work here for you to do."

"What must I do?" said Cadmus.

"Follow the white cow," said the Pythia; "and on the hill where she lies down, you must build a city."

Cadmus did not understand what she meant by this; but she would not speak another word.

"This must be one of her riddles," he said, and he left the temple.

III. THE DRAGON.

When Cadmus went out of the temple, he saw a snow-white cow standing not far from the door. She seemed to be waiting for him, for she looked at him with her large brown eyes, and then turned and walked away. Cadmus thought of what the Pythia had just told him, and so he followed her. All day and all night he walked

49

through a strange wild country where no one lived; and two of the young men who had sailed with Cadmus from his old home were with him.

When the sun rose the next morning, they saw that they were on the top of a beautiful hill, with woods on one side and a grassy meadow on the other. There the cow lay down.

"Here we will build our city," said Cadmus.

Then the young men made a fire of dry sticks, and Cadmus killed the cow. They thought that if they should burn some of her flesh, the smell of it would go up to the sky and be pleasing to Jupiter and the Mighty Folk who lived with him among the clouds; and in this way they hoped to make friends with Jupiter so that he would not hinder them in their work.

But they needed water to wash the flesh and their hands; and so one of the young men went down the hill to find some. He was gone so long that the other young man became uneasy and went after him.

Cadmus waited for them till the fire had burned low. He waited and waited till the sun was high in the sky. He called and shouted, but no one answered him. At last he took his sword in his hand and went down to see what was the matter.

He followed the path which his friends had taken, and soon came to a fine stream of cold water at the foot of a hill. He saw something move among the bushes which grew near it. It was a fierce dragon, waiting to spring upon him. There was blood on the grass and leaves, and it was not hard to guess what had become of the two young men.

The beast sprang at Cadmus, and tried to seize him with its sharp claws. But Cadmus leaped quickly aside and struck it in the neck with his long sword. A great stream of black blood gushed out, and the dragon soon fell to the ground dead. Cadmus had seen many fearful sights, but never anything so dreadful as this beast. He had never been in so great danger before. He sat down on the ground and trembled; and, all the time, he was weeping for his two friends. How now was he to build a city, with no one to help him?

IV. THE CITY.

While Cadmus was still weeping he was surprised to hear some one calling him. He stood up and looked around. On the hillside before him was a tall woman who had a helmet on her head and a shield in her hand. Her eyes were gray, and her face, though not beautiful, was very noble. Cadmus knew at once that she was

Imagery

Athena, the queen of the air-she who gives wisdom to men.

Athena told Cadmus that he must take out the teeth of the dragon and sow them in the ground. He thought that would be a queer kind of seed. But she said that if he would do this, he would soon have men enough to help him build his city; and, before he could say a word, she had gone out of his sight.

018

SOON THEY BEGAN TO FIGHT AMONG THEMSELVES.

The dragon had a great many teeth-so many that when Cadmus had taken them out they filled his helmet heaping full. The next thing was to find a good place to sow them. Just as he turned away from the stream, he saw a yoke of oxen standing a little way off. He went to them and found that they were hitched to a plow. What more could he want? The ground in the meadow was soft and black, and he drove the plow up and down, making long furrows as he went. Then he dropped the teeth, one by one, into the furrows and covered them over with the rich soil. When he had sown all of them in this way, he sat down on the hillside and watched to see what would happen.

In a little while the soil in the furrows began to stir. Then, at every place that a tooth had been dropped, something bright grew up. It was a brass helmet. The helmets pushed their way up, and soon the faces of men were seen underneath, then their shoulders, then their arms, then their bodies; and then, before Cadmus could think, a thousand warriors leaped out of the furrows and shook off the black earth which was clinging to them. Every man was clothed in a suit of brass armor; and every one had a long spear in his right hand and a shield in his left.

Cadmus was frightened when he saw the strange crop which had grown up from the dragon's teeth. The men looked so fierce that he feared they would kill him if they saw him. He hid himself behind his plow and then began to throw stones at them. The warriors did not know where the stones came from, but each thought that his neighbor had struck him. Soon they began to fight among themselves. Man after man was killed, and in a little while only five were left alive. Then Cadmus ran towards them and called out:

"Hold! Stop fighting! You are my men, and must come with me. We will build a city here."

The men obeyed him. They followed Cadmus to the top of the hill; and they were such good workmen that in a few days they had built a house on the spot where the cow had lain down.

After that they built other houses, and people came to live in them. They called the town Cadmeia, after Cadmus who was its first king. But when the place had grown to be a large city, it was known by the name of Thebes.

Cadmus was a wise king. The Mighty Folk who lived with Jupiter amid the clouds were well pleased with him and helped him in more ways than one. After a while he married Harmonia, the beautiful daughter of Mars. All the Mighty Ones were at the wedding; and Athena gave the bride a wonderful necklace about which you may learn something more at another time.

But the greatest thing that Cadmus did is yet to be told. He was the first schoolmaster of the Greeks, and taught them the letters which were used in his own country across the sea. They called the first of these letters alpha and the second beta, and that is why men speak of the alphabet to this day. And when the Greeks had learned the alphabet from Cadmus, they soon began to read and write, and to make beautiful and useful books.

As for the maiden Europa, she was carried safe over the sea to a distant shore. She may have been happy in the new, strange land to which she was taken-I cannot tell; but she never heard of friends or home again. Whether it was really Jupiter in the form of a bull that carried her away, nobody knows. It all happened so long ago that there may have been some mistake about the story; and I should not think it strange if it were a sea robber who stole her from her home, and a swift ship with white sails that bore her away. Of one thing I am very sure: she was loved so well by all who knew her that the great unknown country to which she was taken has been called after her name ever since-Europe.

019

THE QUEST OF MEDUSA'S HEAD.

I. THE WOODEN CHEST.

There was a king of Argos who had but one child, and that child was a girl. If he had had a son, he would have trained him up to be a brave man and great king; but he did not know what to do with this fair-haired daughter. When he saw her growing up to be tall and slender and wise, he wondered if, after all, he would have to die some time and leave his lands and his gold and his kingdom to her. So he sent to Delphi and asked the Pythia about it. The Pythia told him that he would not only have to die some time, but that the son of his daughter would cause his death.

This frightened the king very much, and he tried to think of some plan by which he could keep the Pythia's words from coming true. At last he made up his mind that he would build a prison for his daughter and keep her in it all her life. So he called his workmen and had them dig a deep round hole in the ground, and in this hole they built a house of brass which had but one room and no door at all, but only a small window at the top. When it was finished, the king put the maiden, whose name was Danaë, into it; and with her he put her nurse and her toys and her pretty dresses and everything that he thought she would need to make her happy.

"Now we shall see that the Pythia does not always tell the truth," he said.

So Danaë was kept shut up in the prison of brass. She had no one to talk to but her old nurse; and she never saw the land or the sea, but only the blue sky above the open window and now and then a white cloud sailing across. Day after day she sat under the window and wondered why her father kept her in that lonely place, and whether he would ever come and take her out. I do not know how many years passed by, but Danaë grew fairer every day, and by and by she was no longer a child, but a tall and beautiful woman; and Jupiter amid the clouds looked down and saw her and loved her.

One day it seemed to her that the sky opened and a shower of gold fell through the window into the room; and when the blinding shower had ceased, a noble young man stood smiling before her. She did not know-nor do I-that it was mighty Jupiter who had thus come down in the rain; but she thought that he was a brave prince who had come from over the sea to take her out of her prison-house.

After that he came often, but always as a tall and handsome youth; and by and by they were married, with only the nurse at the wedding feast, and Danaë was so happy that she was no longer lonesome even when he was away. But one day when he climbed out through the narrow window there was a great flash of light, and she never saw him again.

Not long afterwards a babe was born to Danaë, a smiling boy whom she named Perseus. For four years she and the nurse kept him hidden, and not even the women who brought their food to the window knew about him. But one day the king chanced to be passing by and heard the child's prattle. When he learned the truth, he was very much alarmed, for he thought that now, in spite of all that he had done, the words of the Pythia might come true.

The only sure way to save himself would be to put the child to death before he was old enough to do any harm. But when he had taken the little Perseus and his mother out of the prison and had seen how helpless the child was, he could not bear the thought of having him killed outright. For the king, although a great coward, was really a kind-hearted man and did not like to see anything suffer pain. Yet something must be done.

So he bade his servants make a wooden chest that was roomy and watertight and strong; and when it was done, he put Danaë and the child into it and had it taken

54

far out to sea and left there to be tossed about by the waves. He thought that in this way he would rid himself of both daughter and grandson without seeing them die; for surely the chest would sink after a while, or else the winds would cause it to drift to some strange shore so far away that they could never come back to Argos again.

All day and all night and then another day, fair Danaë and her child drifted over the sea. The waves rippled and played before and around the floating chest, the west wind whistled cheerily, and the sea birds circled in the air above; and the child was not afraid, but dipped his hands in the curling waves and laughed at the merry breeze and shouted back at the screaming birds.

Personification

+ Imagery

But on the second night all was changed. A storm arose, the sky was black, the billows were mountain high, the winds roared fearfully, yet through it all the child slept soundly in his mother's arms. And Danaë sang over him this song: "Sleep, sleep, dear child, and take your rest
Upon your troubled mother's breast;
For you can lie without one fear

Imagery

Personification

Of dreadful danger lurking near.

Wrapped in soft robes and warmly sleeping,
You do not hear your mother weeping;
You do not see the mad waves leaping,
Nor heed the winds their vigils keeping.

The stars are hid, the night is drear,
The waves beat high, the storm is here;
But you can sleep, my darling child,
And know naught of the uproar wild."

At last the morning of the third day came, and the chest was tossed upon the sandy shore of a strange island where there were green fields and, beyond them, a little town. A man who happened to be walking near the shore saw it and dragged it far up on the beach. Then he looked inside, and there he saw the beautiful lady and the little boy. He helped them out and led them just as they were to his own house, where he cared for them very kindly. And when Danaë had told him her story, he bade her feel no more fear; for they might have a home with him as long as they should choose to stay, and he would be a true friend to them both.

II. THE MAGIC SLIPPERS.

So Danaë and her son stayed in the house of the kind man who had saved them from the sea. Years passed by, and Perseus grew up to be a tall young man, handsome, and brave, and strong. The king of the island, when he saw Danaë, was so pleased with her beauty that he wanted her to become his wife. But he was a dark, cruel man, and she did not like him at all; so she told him that she would not marry him. The king thought that Perseus was to blame for this, and that if he could find some excuse to send the young man on a far journey, he might force Danaë to have him whether she wished or not.

One day he called all the young men of his country together and told them that he was soon to be wedded to the queen of a certain land beyond the sea. Would not each of them bring him a present to be given to her father? For in those times it was the rule, that when any man was about to be married, he must offer costly gifts to the father of the bride.

"What kind of presents do you want?" said the young men.

"Horses," he answered; for he knew that Perseus had no horse.

"Why don't you ask for something worth the having?" said Perseus; for he was vexed at the way in which the king was treating him. "Why don't you ask for Medusa's head, for example?"

57

"Medusa's head it shall be!" cried the king. "These young men may give me horses, but you shall bring Medusa's head."

"I will bring it," said Perseus; and he went away in anger, while his young friends laughed at him because of his foolish words.

What was this Medusa's head which he had so rashly promised to bring? His mother had often told him about Medusa. Far, far away, on the very edge of the world, there lived three strange monsters, sisters, called Gorgons. They had the bodies and faces of women, but they had wings of gold, and terrible claws of brass, and hair that was full of living serpents. They were so awful to look upon, that no man could bear the sight of them, but whoever saw their faces was turned to stone. Two of these monsters had charmed lives, and no weapon could ever do them harm; but the youngest, whose name was Medusa, might be killed, if indeed anybody could find her and could give the fatal stroke.

When Perseus went away from the king's palace, he began to feel sorry that he had spoken so rashly. For how should he ever make good his promise and do the king's bidding? He did not know which way to go to find the Gorgons, and he had no weapon with which to slay the terrible Medusa. But at any rate he would never show his face to the king again, unless he could bring the head of terror with him. He went down to the shore and stood looking out over the sea towards Argos, his native land; and while he looked, the sun went down, and the moon arose, and a soft wind came blowing from the west. Then, all at once, two persons, a man and a woman, stood before him. Both were tall and noble. The man looked like a prince; and there were wings on his cap and on his feet, and he carried a winged staff, around which two golden serpents were twined.

He asked Perseus what was the matter; and the young man told him how the king had treated him, and all about the rash words which he had spoken. Then the lady spoke to him very kindly; and he noticed that, although she was not beautiful, she had most wonderful gray eyes, and a stern but lovable face and a queenly form. And she told him not to fear, but to go out boldly in quest of the Gorgons, for she would help him obtain the terrible head of Medusa.

"But I have no ship, and how shall I go?" said Perseus.

"You shall don my winged slippers," said the strange prince, "and they will bear you over sea and land."

"Shall I go north, or south, or east, or west?" asked Perseus.

"I will tell you," said the tall lady. "You must go first to the three Gray Sisters, who live beyond the frozen sea in the far, far north. They have a secret which nobody knows, and you must force them to tell it to you. Ask them where you shall find the three Maidens who guard the golden apples of the West; and when they shall have told you, turn about and go straight thither. The Maidens will give you three things, without which you can never obtain the terrible head; and they will show you how to wing your way across the western ocean to the edge of the world where lies the home of the Gorgons."

Then the man took off his winged slippers, and put them on the feet of Perseus; and the woman whispered to him to be off at once, and to fear nothing, but be bold and true. And Perseus knew that she was none other than Athena, the queen of the air, and that her companion was Mercury, the lord of the summer clouds. But before he could thank them for their kindness, they had vanished in the dusky twilight.

Then he leaped into the air to try the Magic Slippers.

III. THE GRAY SISTERS.

Swifter than an eagle, Perseus flew up towards the sky. Then he turned, and the Magic Slippers bore him over the sea straight towards the north. On and on he went, and soon the sea was passed; and he came to a famous land, where there were cities and towns and many people. And then he flew over a range of snowy mountains, beyond which were mighty forests and a vast plain where many rivers wandered, seeking for the sea. And farther on was another range of mountains; and then there were frozen marshes and a wilderness of snow, and after all the sea again,-but a sea of ice. On and on he winged his way, among toppling icebergs and over frozen billows and through air which the sun never warmed, and at last he came to the cavern where the three Gray Sisters dwelt.

These three creatures were so old that they had forgotten their own age, and nobody could count the years which they had lived. The long hair which covered their heads had been gray since they were born; and they had among them only a single eye and a single tooth which they passed back and forth from one to another. Perseus heard them mumbling and crooning in their dreary home, and he stood very still and listened.

"We know a secret which even the Great Folk who live on the mountain top can never learn; don't we, sisters?" said one.

"Ha! ha! That we do, that we do!" chattered the others.

"Give me the tooth, sister, that I may feel young and handsome again," said the one nearest to Perseus.

"And give me the eye that I may look out and see what is going on in the busy world," said the sister who sat next to her.

"Ah, yes, yes, yes, yes!" mumbled the third, as she took the tooth and the eye and reached them blindly towards the others.

Then, quick as thought, Perseus leaped forward and snatched both of the precious things from her hand.

"Where is the tooth? Where is the eye?" screamed the two, reaching out their long arms and groping here and there. "Have you dropped them, sister? Have you lost them?"

Perseus laughed as he stood in the door of their cavern and saw their distress and terror.

"I have your tooth and your eye," he said, "and you shall never touch them again until you tell me your secret. Where are the Maidens who keep the golden apples of the Western Land? Which way shall I go to find them?"

"You are young, and we are old," said the Gray Sisters; "pray, do not deal so cruelly with us. Pity us, and give us our eye."

Then they wept and pleaded and coaxed and threatened. But Perseus stood a little way off and taunted them; and they moaned and mumbled and shrieked, as they found that their words did not move him.

"Sisters, we must tell him," at last said one.

"Ah, yes, we must tell him," said the others. "We must part with the secret to save our eye."

And then they told him how he should go to reach the Western Land, and what road he should follow to find the Maidens who kept the golden apples. When they had made everything plain to him Perseus gave them back their eye and their tooth.

"Ha! ha!" they laughed; "now the golden days of youth have come again!" And, from that day to this, no man has ever seen the three Gray Sisters, nor does any one know what became of them. But the winds still whistle through their cheerless cave, and the cold waves murmur on the shore of the wintry sea, and the ice mountains topple and crash, and no sound of living creature is heard in all that desolate land.

IV. THE WESTERN MAIDENS.

60

As for Perseus, he leaped again into the air, and the Magic Slippers bore him southward with the speed of the wind. Very soon he left the frozen sea behind him and came to a sunny land, where there were green forests and flowery meadows and hills and valleys, and at last a pleasant garden where were all kinds of blossoms and fruits. He knew that this was the famous Western Land, for the Gray Sisters had told him what he should see there. So he alighted and walked among the trees until he came to the center of the garden. There he saw the three Maidens of the West dancing around a tree which was full of golden apples, and singing as they danced. For the wonderful tree with its precious fruit belonged to Juno, the queen of earth and sky; it had been given to her as a wedding gift, and it was the duty of the Maidens to care for it and see that no one touched the golden apples.

Perseus stopped and listened to their song: "We sing of the old, we sing of the new,-
Our joys are many, our sorrows are few;
Singing, dancing,
All hearts entrancing,
We wait to welcome the good and the true.

The daylight is waning, the evening is here,
The sun will soon set, the stars will appear.
Singing, dancing,
All hearts entrancing,
We wait for the dawn of a glad new year.

The tree shall wither, the apples shall fall,
Sorrow shall come, and death shall call,
Alarming, grieving,
All hearts deceiving,-
But hope shall abide to comfort us all.

Soon the tale shall be told, the song shall be sung,
The bow shall be broken, the harp unstrung,
Alarming, grieving,
All hearts deceiving,
Till every joy to the winds shall be flung.

But a new tree shall spring from the roots of the old,
And many a blossom its leaves shall unfold,
Cheering, gladdening,
With joy maddening,-
For its boughs shall be laden with apples of gold."
020

61

PERSEUS STOPPED AND LISTENED TO THEIR SONG.

Then Perseus went forward and spoke to the Maidens. They stopped singing, and stood still as if in alarm. But when they saw the Magic Slippers on his feet, they ran to him, and welcomed him to the Western Land and to their garden.

"We knew that you were coming," they said, "for the winds told us. But why do you come?"

Perseus told them of all that had happened to him since he was a child, and of his quest of Medusa's head; and he said that he had come to ask them to give him three things to help him in his fight with the Gorgons.

The Maidens answered that they would give him not three things, but four. Then one of them gave him a sharp sword, which was crooked like a sickle, and which she fastened to the belt at his waist; and another gave him a shield, which was brighter than any looking-glass you ever saw; and the third gave him a magic pouch, which she hung by a long strap over his shoulder.

"These are three things which you must have in order to obtain Medusa's head; and now here is a fourth, for without it your quest must be in vain." And they gave him a magic cap, the Cap of Darkness; and when they had put it upon his head, there was no creature on the earth or in the sky-no, not even the Maidens themselves-that could see him.

When at last he was arrayed to their liking, they told him where he would find the Gorgons, and what he should do to obtain the terrible head and escape alive. Then they kissed him and wished him good luck, and bade him hasten to do the dangerous deed. And Perseus donned the Cap of Darkness, and sped away and away towards the farthermost edge of the earth; and the three Maidens went back to their tree to sing and to dance and to guard the golden apples until the old world should become young again.

V. THE DREADFUL GORGONS.

With the sharp sword at his side and the bright shield upon his arm, Perseus flew bravely onward in search of the dreadful Gorgons; but he had the Cap of Darkness upon his head, and you could no more have seen him than you can see the wind. He flew so swiftly that it was not long until he had crossed the mighty ocean which encircles the earth, and had come to the sunless land which lies beyond; and then he knew, from what the Maidens had told him, that the lair of the Gorgons could not be far away.

He heard a sound as of some one breathing heavily, and he looked around sharply to see where it came from. Among the foul weeds which grew close to the bank of a muddy river there was something which glittered in the pale light. He flew a little nearer; but he did not dare to look straight forward, lest he should all at once meet the gaze of a Gorgon, and be changed into stone. So he turned around, and held the shining shield before him in such a way that by looking into it he could see objects behind him as in a mirror.

Ah, what a dreadful sight it was! Half hidden among the weeds lay the three monsters, fast asleep, with their golden wings folded about them. Their brazen claws were stretched out as though ready to seize their prey; and their shoulders were covered with sleeping snakes. The two largest of the Gorgons lay with their heads tucked under their wings as birds hide their heads when they go to sleep. But the third, who lay between them, slept with her face turned up towards the sky; and Perseus knew that she was Medusa.

Very stealthily he went nearer and nearer, always with his back towards the monsters and always looking into his bright shield to see where to go. Then he drew his sharp sword and, dashing quickly downward, struck a back blow, so sure, so swift, that the head of Medusa was cut from her shoulders and the black blood gushed like a river from her neck. Quick as thought he thrust the terrible head into his magic pouch and leaped again into the air, and flew away with the speed of the wind.

Then the two older Gorgons awoke, and rose with dreadful screams, and spread their great wings, and dashed after him. They could not see him, for the Cap of Darkness hid him from even their eyes; but they scented the blood of the head which he carried in the pouch, and like hounds in the chase, they followed him, sniffing the air. And as he flew through the clouds he could hear their dreadful cries and the clatter of their golden wings and the snapping of their horrible jaws. But the Magic Slippers were faster than any wings, and in a little while the monsters were left far behind, and their cries were heard no more; and Perseus flew on alone.

VI. THE GREAT SEA BEAST.

Perseus soon crossed the ocean and came again to the Land of the West. Far below him he could see the three Maidens dancing around the golden tree; but he did not stop, for, now that he had the head of Medusa safe in the pouch at his side, he must hasten home. Straight east he flew over the great sea, and after a time he came to a country where there were palm trees and pyramids and a great river flowing from the south. Here, as he looked down, a strange sight met his eyes: he saw a beautiful girl chained to a rock by the seashore, and far away a huge sea beast swimming towards her to devour her. Quick as thought, he flew down and spoke to her; but, as she could not see him for the Cap of Darkness which he wore, his voice only frightened her.

Then Perseus took off his cap, and stood upon the rock; and when the girl saw him with his long hair and wonderful eyes and laughing face, she thought him the handsomest young man in the world.

"Oh, save me! save me!" she cried as she reached out her arms towards him.

Perseus drew his sharp sword and cut the chain which held her, and then lifted her high up upon the rock. But by this time the sea monster was close at hand, lashing the water with his tail and opening his wide jaws as though he would swallow not only Perseus and the young girl, but even the rock on which they were standing. He was a terrible fellow, and yet not half so terrible as the Gorgon. As he came roaring towards the shore, Perseus lifted the head of Medusa from his pouch and held it up; and when the beast saw the dreadful face he stopped short and was turned into stone; and men say that the stone beast may be seen in that selfsame spot to this day.

Then Perseus slipped the Gorgon's head back into the pouch and hastened to speak with the young girl whom he had saved. She told him that her name was Andromeda, and that she was the daughter of the king of that land. She said that her mother, the queen, was very beautiful and very proud of her beauty; and every day she went down to the seashore to look at her face as it was pictured in the quiet water; and she had boasted that not even the nymphs who live in the sea were as handsome as she. When the sea nymphs heard about this, they were very angry and asked great Neptune, the king of the sea, to punish the queen for her pride. So Neptune sent a sea monster to crush the king's ships and kill the cattle along the shore and break down all the fishermen's huts. The people were so much distressed that they sent at last to ask the Pythia what they should do; and the Pythia said that there was only one way to save the land from destruction,-that they must give the king's daughter, Andromeda, to the monster to be devoured.

The king and the queen loved their daughter very dearly, for she was their only child; and for a long time they refused to do as the Pythia had told them. But day after day the monster laid waste the land, and threatened to destroy not only the farms, but the towns; and so they were forced in the end to give up Andromeda to save their country. This, then, was why she had been chained to the rock by the shore and left there to perish in the jaws of the beast.

While Perseus was yet talking with Andromeda, the king and the queen and a great company of people came down the shore, weeping and tearing their hair; for they were sure that by this time the monster had devoured his prey. But when they saw her alive and well, and learned that she had been saved by the handsome young man who stood beside her, they could hardly hold themselves for joy. And

64

Perseus was so delighted with Andromeda's beauty that he almost forgot his quest which was not yet finished; and when the king asked him what he should give him as a reward for saving Andromeda's life, he said:

"Give her to me for my wife."

This pleased the king very much; and so, on the seventh day, Perseus and Andromeda were married, and there was a great feast in the king's palace, and everybody was merry and glad. And the two young people lived happily for some time in the land of palms and pyramids; and, from the sea to the mountains, nothing was talked about but the courage of Perseus and the beauty of Andromeda.

021

THE KING SAW IT AND WAS TURNED INTO STONE

VII. THE TIMELY RESCUE.

But Perseus had not forgotten his mother; and so, one fine summer day, he and Andromeda sailed in a beautiful ship to his own home; for the Magic Slippers could not carry both him and his bride through the air. The ship came to land at the very spot where the wooden chest had been cast so many years before; and Perseus and his bride walked through the fields towards the town.

Now, the wicked king of that land had never ceased trying to persuade Danaë to become his wife; but she would not listen to him, and the more he pleaded and threatened, the more she disliked him. At last when he found that she could not be made to have him, he declared that he would kill her; and on this very morning he had started out, sword in hand, to take her life.

So, as Perseus and Andromeda came into the town, whom should they meet but his mother fleeing to the altar of Jupiter, and the king following after, intent on killing her? Danaë was so frightened that she did not see Perseus, but ran right on towards the only place of safety. For it was a law of that land that not even the king should be allowed to harm any one who took refuge on the altar of Jupiter.

When Perseus saw the king rushing like a madman after his mother, he threw himself before him and bade him stop. But the king struck at him furiously with his sword. Perseus caught the blow on his shield, and at the same moment took the head of Medusa from his magic pouch.

"I promised to bring you a present, and here it is!" he cried.

The king saw it, and was turned into stone, just as he stood, with his sword uplifted and that terrible look of anger and passion in his face.

The people of the island were glad when they learned what had happened, for no one loved the wicked king. They were glad, too, because Perseus had come home again, and had brought with him his beautiful wife, Andromeda. So, after they had talked the matter over among themselves, they went to him and asked him to be their king. But he thanked them, and said that he would rule over them for one day only, and that then he would give the kingdom to another, so that he might take his mother back to her home and her kindred in distant Argos.

On the morrow therefore, he gave the kingdom to the kind man who had saved his mother and himself from the sea; and then he went on board his ship, with Andromeda and Danaë, and sailed away across the sea towards Argos.

VIII. THE DEADLY QUOIT.

When Danaë's old father, the king of Argos, heard that a strange ship was coming over the sea with his daughter and her son on board, he was in great distress; for he remembered what the Pythia had foretold about his death. So, without waiting to see the vessel, he left his palace in great haste and fled out of the country.

"My daughter's son cannot kill me if I will keep out of his way," he said.

But Perseus had no wish to harm him; and he was very sad when he learned that his poor grandfather had gone away in fear and without telling any one where he was going. The people of Argos welcomed Danaë to her old home; and they were very proud of her handsome son, and begged that he would stay in their city, so that he might some time become their king.

It happened soon afterwards that the king of a certain country not far away was holding games and giving prizes to the best runners and leapers and quoit throwers. And Perseus went thither to try his strength with the other young men of the land; for if he should be able to gain a prize, his name would become known all over the world. No one in that country knew who he was, but all wondered at his noble stature and his strength and skill; and it was easy enough for him to win all the prizes.

One day, as he was showing what he could do, he threw a heavy quoit a great deal farther than any had been thrown before. It fell in the crowd of lookers-on, and struck a stranger who was standing there. The stranger threw up his hands and sank upon the ground; and when Perseus ran to help him, he saw that he was dead. Now this man was none other than Danaë's father, the old king of Argos. He had fled from his kingdom to save his life, and in doing so had only met his death.

66

Perseus was overcome with grief, and tried in every way to pay honor to the memory of the unhappy king. The kingdom of Argos was now rightfully his own, but he could not bear to take it after having killed his grandfather. So he was glad to exchange with another king who ruled over two rich cities, not far away, called Mycenae and Tiryns. And he and Andromeda lived happily in Mycenae for many years.

022

THE STORY OF ATALANTA

I. THE BEAR ON THE MOUNTAIN.

In a sunny land in Greece called Arcadia there lived a king and a queen who had no children. They wanted very much to have a son who might live to rule over Arcadia when the king was dead, and so, as the years went by, they prayed to great Jupiter on the mountain top that he would send them a son. After a while a child was born to them, but it was a little girl. The father was in a great rage with Jupiter and everybody else.

"What is a girl good for?" he said. "She can never do anything but sing, and spin, and spend money. If the child had been a boy, he might have learned to do many things,-to ride, and to hunt, and to fight in the wars,-and by and by he would have been king of Arcadia. But this girl can never be a king."

Then he called to one of his men and bade him take the babe out to a mountain where there was nothing but rocks and thick woods, and leave it there to be eaten up by the wild bears that lived in the caves and thickets. It would be the easiest way, he said, to get rid of the useless little creature.

The man carried the child far up on the mountain side and laid it down on a bed of moss in the shadow of a great rock. The child stretched out its baby hands towards him and smiled, but he turned away and left it there, for he did not dare to disobey the king.

For a whole night and a whole day the babe lay on its bed of moss, wailing for its mother; but only the birds among the trees heard its pitiful cries. At last it grew so weak for want of food that it could only moan and move its head a little from side to side. It would have died before another day if nobody had cared for it.

Just before dark on the second evening, a she-bear came strolling down the mountain side from her den. She was out looking for her cubs, for some hunters had stolen them that very day while she was away from home. She heard the moans of the little babe, and wondered if it was not one of her lost cubs; and when she saw it lying so helpless on the moss she went to it and looked at it kindly. Was it possible that a little bear could be changed into a pretty babe with fat white hands and with a beautiful gold chain around its neck? The old bear did not know; and as the child looked at her with its bright black eyes, she growled softly and licked its face with her warm tongue and then lay down beside it, just as she would have done with her own little cubs. The babe was too young to feel afraid, and it cuddled close to the old bear and felt that it had found a friend. After a while it fell asleep; but the bear guarded it until morning and then went down the mountain side to look for food.

In the evening, before dark, the bear came again and carried the child to her own den under the shelter of a rock where vines and wild flowers grew; and every day after that she came and gave the child food and played with it. And all the bears on the mountain learned about the wonderful cub that had been found, and came to see it; but not one of them offered to harm it. And the little girl grew fast and became strong, and after a while could walk and run among the trees and rocks and brambles on the round top of the mountain; but her bear mother would not allow her to wander far from the den beneath the rock where the vines and the wild flowers grew.

One day some hunters came up the mountain to look for game, and one of them pulled aside the vines which grew in front of the old bear's home. He was surprised to see the beautiful child lying on the grass and playing with the flowers which she had gathered. But at sight of him she leaped to her feet and bounded away like a frightened deer. She led the hunters a fine chase among the trees and rocks; but there were a dozen of them, and it was not long till they caught her.

The hunters had never taken such game as that before, and they were so well satisfied that they did not care to hunt any more that day. The child struggled and fought as hard as she knew how, but it was of no use. The hunters carried her down the mountain, and took her to the house where they lived on the other side of the forest. At first she cried all the time, for she sadly missed the bear that had been a mother to her so long. But the hunters made a great pet of her, and gave her many pretty things to play with, and were very kind; and it was not long till she began to like her new home.

The hunters named her Atalanta, and when she grew older, they made her a bow and arrows, and taught her how to shoot; and they gave her a light spear, and showed her how to carry it and how to hurl it at the game or at an enemy. Then they took her with them when they went hunting, and there was nothing in the world that pleased her so much as roaming through the woods and running after the deer and other wild animals. Her feet became very swift, so that she could run faster than any of the men; and her arms were so strong and her eyes so sharp and true that with her arrow or her spear she never missed the mark. And she grew up to be very tall and graceful, and was known throughout all Arcadia as the fleet-footed huntress.

II. THE BRAND ON THE HEARTH.

Now, not very far from the land of Arcadia there was a little city named Calydon. It lay in the midst of rich wheat fields and fruitful vineyards; but beyond the vineyards there was a deep dense forest where many wild beasts lived. The king of Calydon was named OEneus, and he dwelt in a white palace with his wife Althea and his boys and girls. His kingdom was so small that it was not much trouble to govern it, and so he spent the most of his time in hunting or in plowing or in looking after his grape vines. He was said to be a very brave man, and he was the friend of all the great heroes of that heroic time.

The two daughters of OEneus and Althea were famed all over the world for their beauty; and one of them was the wife of the hero Hercules, who had freed Prometheus from his chains, and done many other mighty deeds. The six sons of OEneus and Althea were noble, handsome fellows; but the noblest and handsomest of them all was Meleager, the youngest.

When Meleager was a tiny babe only seven days old, a strange thing happened in the white palace of the king. Queen Althea awoke in the middle of the night, and saw a fire blazing on the hearth. She wondered what it could mean; and she lay quite still by the side of the babe, and looked and listened. Three strange women were standing by the hearth. They were tall, and two of them were beautiful, and the faces of all were stern. Althea knew at once that they were the Fates who give gifts of some kind to every child that is born, and who say whether his life shall be a happy one or full of sadness and sorrow.

"What shall we give to this child?" said the eldest and sternest of the three strangers. Her name was Atropos, and she held a pair of sharp shears in her hand.

"I give him a brave heart," said the youngest and fairest. Her name was Clotho, and she held a distaff full of flax, from which she was spinning a golden thread.

"And I give him a gentle, noble mind," said the dark-haired one, whose name was Lachesis. She gently drew out the thread which Clotho spun, and turning to stern Atropos, said: "Lay aside those shears, sister, and give the child your gift."

"I give him life until this brand shall be burned to ashes," was the answer; and Atropos took a small stick of wood and laid it on the burning coals.

The three sisters waited till the stick was ablaze, and then they were gone. Althea sprang up quickly. She saw nothing but the fire on the hearth and the stick burning slowly away. She made haste to pour water upon the blaze, and when every spark was put out, she took the charred stick and put it into a strong chest where she kept her treasures, and locked it up.

"I know that the child's life is safe," she said, "so long as that stick is kept unburned."

And so, as the years went by, Meleager grew up to be a brave young man, so gentle and noble that his name became known in every land of Greece. He did many daring deeds and, with other heroes, went on a famous voyage across the seas in search of a marvelous fleece of gold; and when he returned to Calydon the people declared that he was the worthiest of the sons of OEneus to become their king.

III. THE GIFTS ON THE ALTARS.

Now it happened one summer that the vineyards of Calydon were fuller of grapes than they had ever been before, and there was so much wheat in the fields that the people did not know what to do with it.

"I will tell you what to do," said King OEneus. "We will have a thanksgiving day, and we will give some of the grain and some of the fruit to the Mighty Beings who sit among the clouds on the mountain top. For it is from them that the sunshine and the fair weather and the moist winds and the warm rains have come; and without their aid we could never have had so fine a harvest."

The very next day the king and the people of Calydon went out into the fields and vineyards to offer up their thank offerings. Here and there they built little altars of turf and stones and laid dry grass and twigs upon them; and then on top of the twigs they put some of the largest bunches of grapes and some of the finest heads of wheat, which they thought would please the Mighty Beings who had sent them so great plenty.

There was one altar for Ceres, who had shown men how to sow grain, and one for Bacchus, who had told them about the grape, and one for wing-footed Mercury, who comes in the clouds, and one for Athena, the queen of the air, and one for the keeper of the winds, and one for the giver of light, and one for the driver of the golden sun car, and one for the king of the sea, and one-which was the largest of all-for Jupiter, the mighty thunderer who sits upon the mountain top and rules the world. And when everything was ready, King OEneus gave the word, and fire was touched to the grass and the twigs upon the altars; and the grapes and the wheat that had been laid there were burned up. Then the people shouted and danced, for they fancied that in that way the thank offerings were sent right up to Ceres and Bacchus and Mercury and Athena and all the rest. And in the evening they went home with glad hearts, feeling that they had done right.

But they had forgotten one of the Mighty Beings. They had not raised any altar to Diana, the fair huntress and queen of the woods, and they had not offered her a single grape or a single grain of wheat. They had not intended to slight her; but, to tell the truth, there were so many others that they had never once thought about her.

I do not suppose that Diana cared anything at all for the fruit or the grain; but it made her very angry to think that she should be forgotten.
"I'll show them that I am not to be slighted in this way," she said.
All went well, however, until the next summer; and the people of Calydon were very happy, for it looked as though there would be a bigger harvest than ever.

"I tell you," said old King OEneus, looking over his fields and his vineyards, "it pays to give thanks. We'll have another thanksgiving as soon as the grapes begin to ripen."

But even then he did not think of Diana.

The very next day the largest and fiercest wild boar that anybody had ever seen came rushing out of the forest. He had two long tusks which stuck far out of his mouth on either side and were as sharp as knives, and the stiff bristles on his back were as large and as long as knitting needles. As he went tearing along towards Calydon, champing his teeth and foaming at the mouth, he was a frightful thing to look at, I tell you. Everybody fled before him. He rushed into the wheat fields and tore up all the grain; he went into the vineyards and broke down all the vines; he rooted up all the trees in the orchards; and, when there was nothing else to do, he went into the pasture lands among the hills and killed the sheep that were feeding there. He was so fierce and so fleet of foot that the bravest warrior hardly dared to attack him. His thick skin was proof against arrows and against such spears as the people of Calydon had; and I do not know how many men he killed with those terrible razor tusks of his. For weeks he had pretty much his own way, and the only safe place for anybody was inside of the walls.

When he had laid waste the whole country he went back into the edge of the forest; but the people were so much afraid of him that they lived in dread every day lest he should come again and tear down the gates of the city.

"We must have forgotten somebody when we gave thanks last year," said King OEneus. "Who could it have been?"

And then he thought of Diana.

"Diana, the queen of the chase," said he, "has sent this monster to punish us for

71

forgetting her. I am sure that we shall remember her now as long as we live."

Then he sent messengers into all the countries near Calydon, asking the bravest men and skillfullest hunters to come at a certain time and help him hunt and kill the great wild boar. Very many of these men had been with Meleager in that wonderful voyage in search of the Golden Fleece, and he felt sure they would come.

IV. THE HUNT IN THE FOREST.

When the day came which King OEneus had set, there was a wonderful gathering of men at Calydon. The greatest heroes in the world were there; and every one was fully armed, and expected to have fine sport hunting the terrible wild boar. With the warriors from the south there came a tall maiden armed with bow and arrows and a long hunting spear. It was our friend Atalanta, the huntress.

"My daughters are having a game of ball in the garden," said old King OEneus. "Wouldn't you like to put away your arrows and your spear, and go and play with them?"

Atalanta shook her head and lifted her chin as if in disdain.

"Perhaps you would rather stay with the queen, and look at the women spin and weave," said OEneus.

"No," answered Atalanta, "I am going with the warriors to hunt the wild boar in the forest!"

How all the men opened their eyes! They had never heard of such a thing as a girl going out with heroes to hunt wild boars.

"If she goes, then I will not," said one.

"Nor I, either," said another.

"Nor I," said a third. "Why, the whole world would laugh at us, and we should never hear the end of it."

Several threatened to go home at once; and two brothers of Queen Althea, rude, unmannerly fellows, loudly declared that the hunt was for heroes and not for puny girls.

But Atalanta only grasped her spear more firmly and stood up, tall and straight, in the gateway of the palace. Just then a handsome young man came forward. It was

72

Meleager.

"What's this?" he cried. "Who says that Atalanta shall not go to the hunt? You are afraid that she'll be braver than you-that is all. Pretty heroes you are! Let all such cowards go home at once."

But nobody went, and it was settled then and there that the maiden should have her own way. And yet the brothers of Queen Althea kept on muttering and complaining.

For nine days the heroes and huntsmen feasted in the halls of King OEneus, and early on the tenth they set out for the forest. Soon the great beast was found, and he came charging out upon his foes. The heroes hid behind the trees or climbed up among the branches, for they had not expected to see so terrible a creature. He stood in the middle of a little open space, tearing up the ground with his tusks. The white foam rolled from his mouth, his eyes glistened red like fire, and he grunted so fiercely that the woods and hills echoed with fearful sounds.

023

YOU OUGHT TO HAVE SEEN THE TALL HUNTRESS MAIDEN THEN

Then one of the bravest of the men threw his spear. But that only made the beast fiercer than ever; he charged upon the warrior, caught him before he could save himself, and tore him in pieces with his tusks. Another man ventured too far from his hiding-place and was also overtaken and killed. One of the oldest and noblest of the heroes leveled his spear and threw it with all his force; but it only grazed the boar's tough skin and glanced upward and pierced the heart of a warrior on the other side. The boar was getting the best of the fight.

Atalanta now ran forward and threw her spear. It struck the boar in the back, and a great stream of blood gushed out. A warrior let fly an arrow which put out one of the beast's eyes. Then Meleager rushed up and pierced his heart with his spear. The boar could no longer stand up; but he fought fiercely for some moments, and then rolled over, dead.

The heroes then cut off the beast's head. It was as much as six of them could carry. Then they took the skin from his great body and offered it to Meleager as a prize, because he had given the death wound to the wild boar. But Meleager said:

"It belongs to Atalanta, because it was she who gave him the very first wound." And he gave it to her as the prize of honor.

You ought to have seen the tall huntress maiden then, as she stood among the trees with the boar's skin thrown over her left shoulder and reaching down to her feet.

She had never looked so much like the queen of the woods. But the rude brothers of Queen Althea were vexed to think that a maiden should win the prize, and they began to make trouble. One of them snatched Atalanta's spear from her hand, and dragged the prize from her shoulders, and the other pushed her rudely and bade her go back to Arcadia and live again with the she-bears on the mountain side. All this vexed Meleager, and he tried to make his uncles give back the spear and the prize, and stop their unmannerly talk. But they grew worse and worse, and at last set upon Meleager, and would have killed him if he had not drawn his sword to defend himself. A fight followed, and the rude fellows struck right and left as though they were blind. Soon both were stretched dead upon the ground. Some who did not see the fight said that Meleager killed them, but I would rather believe that they killed each other in their drunken fury.

And now all the company started back to the city. Some carried the boar's huge head, and some the different parts of his body, while others had made biers of the green branches, and bore upon them the dead bodies of those who had been slain. It was indeed a strange procession.

A young man who did not like Meleager, had run on in front and had reached the city before the rest of the company had fairly started. Queen Althea was standing at the door of the palace, and when she saw him she asked what had happened in the forest He told her at once that Meleager had killed her brothers, for he knew that, with all their faults, she loved them very dearly. It was terrible to see her grief. She shrieked, and tore her hair, and rushed wildly about from room to room. Her senses left her, and she did not know what she was doing.

It was the custom at that time for people to avenge the death of their kindred, and her only thought was how to punish the murderer of her brothers. In her madness she forgot that Meleager was her son. Then she thought of the three Fates and of the unburned firebrand which she had locked up in her chest so many years before. She ran and got the stick and threw it into the fire that was burning on the hearth.

It kindled at once, and she watched it as it blazed up brightly. Then it began to turn into ashes, and as the last spark died out, the noble Meleager, who was walking by the side of Atalanta, dropped to the ground dead.

When they carried the news to Althea she said not a word, for then she knew what she had done, and her heart was broken. She turned silently away and went to her own room. When the king came home a few minutes later, he found her dead.

So ended the hunt in the wood of Calydon.

V. THE RACE FOR A WIFE.

After the death of Meleager, Atalanta went back to her old home among the mountains of Arcadia. She was still the swift-footed huntress, and she was never so happy as when in the green woods wandering among the trees or chasing the wild deer. All the world had heard about her, however; and the young heroes in the lands nearest to Arcadia did nothing else but talk about her beauty and her grace and her swiftness of foot and her courage. Of course every one of these young fellows wanted her to become his wife; and she might have been a queen any day if she had only said the word, for the richest king in Greece would have been glad to marry her. But she cared nothing for any of the young men, and she liked the freedom of the green woods better than all the fine things she might have had in a palace.

The young men would not take "No!" for an answer, however. They could not believe that she really meant it, and so they kept coming and staying until the woods of Arcadia were full of them, and there was no getting along with them at all. So, when she could think of no other way to get rid of them, Atalanta called them together and said:

"You want to marry me, do you? Well, if any one of you would like to run a race with me from this mountain to the bank of the river over there, he may do so; and I will be the wife of the one who outruns me."

"Agreed! agreed!" cried all the young fellows.

"But, listen!" she said. "Whoever tries this race must also agree that if I outrun him, he must lose his life."

Ah, what long faces they all had then! About half of them drew away and went home.

"But won't you give us the start of you a little?" asked the others.

"Oh, yes," she answered. "I will give you the start by a hundred paces. But remember, if I overtake any one before he reaches the river, he shall lose his head that very day."

Several others now found that they were in ill health or that business called them home; and when they were next looked for, they were not to be found. But a good many who had had some practice in sprinting across the country stayed and made up their minds to try their luck. Could a mere girl outrun such fine fellows as they? Nonsense!

And so it happened that a race was run almost every day. And almost every day some poor fellow lost his head; for the fleetest-footed sprinter in all Greece was

75

overtaken by Atalanta long before he could reach the river bank. But other young men kept coming and coming, and no sooner had one been put out of the way than another took his place.

One day there came from a distant town a handsome, tall young man named Meilanion.

"You'd better not run with me," said Atalanta, "for I shall be sure to overtake you, and that will be the end of you."

"We'll see about that," said Meilanion.

Now Meilanion, before coming to try his chance, had talked with Venus, the queen of love, who lived with Jupiter among the clouds on the mountain top. And he was so handsome and gentle and wise that Venus took pity on him, and gave him three golden apples and told him what to do.

Well, when all was ready for the race, Atalanta tried again to persuade Meilanion not to run, for she also took pity on him.

"I'll be sure to overtake you," she said.

"All right!" said Meilanion, and away he sped; but he had the three golden applies in his pocket.

Atalanta gave him a good start, and then she followed after, as swift as an arrow shot from the bow. Meilanion was not a very fast runner, and it would not be hard for her to overtake him. She thought that she would let him get almost to the goal, for she really pitied him. He heard her coming close behind him; he heard her quick breath as she gained on him very fast. Then he threw one of the golden apples over his shoulder.

Now, if there was anything in the world that Atalanta admired, it was a bright stone or a pretty piece of yellow gold. As the apple fell to the ground she saw how beautiful it was, and she stopped to pick it up; and while she was doing this, Meilanion gained a good many paces. But what of that? In a minute she was as close behind him as ever. And yet, she really did pity him.

Just then Meilanion threw the second apple over his shoulder. It was handsomer and larger than the first, and Atalanta could not bear the thought of allowing some one else to get it. So she stopped to pick it up from among the long grass, where it had fallen. It took somewhat longer to find it than she had expected, and when she looked up again Meilanion was a hundred feet ahead of her. But that was no matter. She could easily overtake him. And yet, how she did pity the foolish young man!

76

Meilanion heard her speeding like the wind behind him. He took the third apple and threw it over to one side of the path where the ground sloped towards the river. Atalanta's quick eye saw that it was far more beautiful than either of the others. If it were not picked up at once it would roll down into the deep water and be lost, and that would never do. She turned aside from her course and ran after it. It was easy enough to overtake the apple, but while she was doing so Meilanion gained upon her again. He was almost to the goal. How she strained every muscle now to overtake him! But, after all, she felt that she did not care very much. He was the handsomest young man that she had ever seen, and he had given her three golden apples. It would be a great pity if he should have to die. And so she let him reach the goal first.

After that, of course, Atalanta became Meilanion's wife. And he took her with him to his distant home, and there they lived happily together for many, many years.

024

THE HORSE AND THE OLIVE

I. FINDING A KING.

On a steep stony hill in Greece there lived in early times a few very poor people who had not yet learned to build houses. They made their homes in little caves which they dug in the earth or hollowed out among the rocks; and their food was the flesh of wild animals, which they hunted in the woods, with now and then a few berries or nuts. They did not even know how to make bows and arrows, but used slings and clubs and sharp sticks for weapons; and the little clothing which they had was made of skins. They lived on the top of the hill, because they were safe there from the savage beasts of the great forest around them, and safe also from the wild men who sometimes roamed through the land. The hill was so steep on every side that there was no way of climbing it save by a single narrow footpath which was always guarded by some one at the top.

One day when the men were hunting in the woods, they found a strange youth whose face was so fair and who was dressed so beautifully that they could hardly believe him to be a man like themselves. His body was so slender and lithe, and he moved so nimbly among the trees, that they fancied him to be a serpent in the guise of a human being; and they stood still in wonder and alarm. The young man spoke to them, but they could not understand a word that he said; then he made signs to them that he was hungry, and they gave him something to eat and were no longer afraid. Had they been like the wild men of the woods, they might have killed him at once. But they wanted their women and children to see the serpent man, as they called him, and hear him talk; and so they took him home with them

77

to the top of the hill. They thought that after they had made a show of him for a few days, they would kill him and offer his body as a sacrifice to the unknown being whom they dimly fancied to have some sort of control over their lives.

But the young man was so fair and gentle that, after they had all taken a look at him, they began to think it would be a great pity to harm him. So they gave him food and treated him kindly; and he sang songs to them and played with their children, and made them happier than they had been for many a day. In a short time he learned to talk in their language; and he told them that his name was Cecrops, and that he had been shipwrecked on the seacoast not far away; and then he told them many strange things about the land from which he had come and to which he would never be able to return. The poor people listened and wondered; and it was not long until they began to love him and to look up to him as one wiser than themselves. Then they came to ask him about everything that was to be done, and there was not one of them who refused to do his bidding.

So Cecrops-the serpent man, as they still called him-became the king of the poor people on the hill. He taught them how to make bows and arrows, and how to set nets for birds, and how to take fish with hooks. He led them against the savage wild men of the woods, and helped them kill the fierce beasts that had been so great a terror to them. He showed them how to build houses of wood and to thatch them with the reeds which grew in the marshes. He taught them how to live in families instead of herding together like senseless beasts as they had always done before. And he told them about great Jupiter and the Mighty Folk who lived amid the clouds on the mountain top.

II. CHOOSING A NAME.

By and by, instead of the wretched caves among the rocks, there was a little town on the top of the hill, with neat houses and a market place; and around it was a strong wall with a single narrow gate just where the footpath began to descend to the plain. But as yet the place had no name.

One morning while the king and his wise men were sitting together in the market place and planning how to make, the town become a rich, strong city, two strangers were seen in the street. Nobody could tell how they came there. The guard at the gate had not seen them; and no man had ever dared to climb the narrow footway without his leave. But there the two strangers stood. One was a man, the other a woman; and they were so tall, and their faces were so grand and noble, that those who saw them stood still and wondered and said not a word.

The man had a robe of purple and green wrapped round his body, and he bore in one hand a strong staff with three sharp spear points at one end. The woman was not beautiful, but she had wonderful gray eyes; and in one hand she carried a spear and in the other a shield of curious workmanship.

"What is the name of this town?" asked the man.

The people stared at him in wonder, and hardly understood his meaning. Then an old man answered and said, "It has no name. We who live on this hill used to be called Cranae; but since King Cecrops came, we have been so busy that we have had no time to think of names."

"Where is this King Cecrops?" asked the woman.

"He is in the market place with the wise men," was the answer.

"Lead us to him at once," said the man.

When Cecrops saw the two strangers coming into the market place, he stood up and waited for them to speak. The man spoke first:

"I am Neptune," said he, "and I rule the sea."

"And I am Athena," said the woman, "and I give wisdom to men."

"I hear that you are planning to make your town become a great city," said Neptune, "and I have come to help you. Give my name to the place, and let me be your protector and patron, and the wealth of the whole world shall be yours. Ships from every land shall bring you merchandise and gold and silver; and you shall be the masters of the sea."

"My uncle makes you fair promises," said Athena; "but listen to me. Give my name to your city, and let me be your patron, and I will give you that which gold cannot buy: I will teach you how to do a thousand things of which you now know nothing. I will make your city my favorite home, and I will give you wisdom that shall sway the minds and hearts of all men until the end of time."

The king bowed, and turned to the people, who had all crowded into the market place. "Which of these mighty ones shall we elect to be the protector and patron of our city?" he asked. "Neptune offers us wealth; Athena promises us wisdom. Which shall we choose?"

"Neptune and wealth!" cried many.

"Athena and wisdom!" cried as many others.

At last when it was plain that the people could not agree, an old man whose advice was always heeded stood up and said:

"These mighty ones have only given us promises, and they have promised things of which we are ignorant. For who among us knows what wealth is or what wisdom is? Now, if they would only give us some real gift, right now and right here, which we can see and handle, we should know better how to choose."

"That is true! that is true!" cried the people.

"Very well, then," said the strangers, "we will each give you a gift, right now and right here, and then you may choose between us."

Neptune gave the first gift. He stood on the highest point of the hill where the rock was bare, and bade the people see his power. He raised his three-pointed spear high in the air, and then brought it down with great force. Lightning flashed, the earth shook, and the rock was split half way down to the bottom of the hill. Then out of the yawning crevice there sprang a wonderful creature, white as milk, with long slender legs, an arching neck, and a mane and tail of silk.

The people had never seen anything like it before, and they thought it a new kind of bear or wolf or wild boar that had come out of the rock to devour them. Some of them ran and hid in their houses, while others climbed upon the wall, and still others grasped their weapons in alarm. But when they saw the creature stand quietly by the side of Neptune, they lost their fear and came closer to see and admire its beauty.

"This is my gift," said Neptune. "This animal will carry your burdens for you; he will draw your chariots; he will pull your wagons and your plows; he will let you sit on his back and will run with you faster than the wind."

025

OUT OF THE YAWNING CREVICE THERE SPRANG A WONDERFUL CREATURE

"What is his name?" asked the king.

"His name is Horse," answered Neptune.

Then Athena came forward. She stood a moment on a green grassy plot where the children of the town liked to play in the evening. Then she drove the point of her spear deep down in the soil. At once the air was filled with music, and out of the earth there sprang a tree with slender branches and dark green leaves and white flowers and violet green fruit.

"This is my gift," said Athena. "This tree will give you food when you are hungry;

it will shelter you from the sun when you are faint; it will beautify your city; and the oil from its fruit will be sought by all the world."

"What is it called?" asked the king.

"It is called Olive," answered Athena.

Then the king and his wise men began to talk about the two gifts.

"I do not see that Horse will be of much use to us," said the old man who had spoken before. "For, as to the chariots and wagons and plows, we have none of them, and indeed do not know what they are; and who among us will ever want to sit on this creature's back and be borne faster than the wind? But Olive will be a thing of beauty and a joy for us and our children forever."

"Which shall we choose?" asked the king, turning to the people.

"Athena has given us the best gift," they all cried, "and we choose Athena and wisdom!"

"Be it so," said the king, "and the name of our city shall be Athens."

From that day the town grew and spread, and soon there was not room on the hilltop for all the people. Then houses were built in the plain around the foot of the hill, and a great road was built to the sea, three miles away; and in all the world there was no city more fair than Athens.

In the old market place on the top of the hill the people built a temple to Athena, the ruins of which may still be seen. The olive tree grew and nourished; and, when you visit Athens, people will show you the very spot where it stood. Many other trees sprang from it, and in time became a blessing both to Greece and to all the other countries round the great sea. As for the horse, he wandered away across the plains towards the north and found a home at last in distant Thessaly beyond the River Peneus. And I have heard it said that all the horses in the world have descended from that one which Neptune brought out of the rock; but of the truth of this story there may be some doubts.

026

THE ADVENTURES OF THESEUS.

I. AEGEUS AND AETHRA.

There was once a king of Athens whose name was AEgeus. He had no son; but he had fifty nephews, and they were waiting for him to die, so that one of them might be king in his stead. They were wild, worthless fellows, and the people of Athens looked forward with dread to the day when the city should be in their power. Yet so long as AEgeus lived they could not do much harm, but were content to spend their time in eating and drinking at the king's table and in quarreling among themselves.

It so happened one summer that AEgeus left his kingdom in the care of the elders of the city and went on a voyage across the Saronic Sea to the old and famous city of Troezen, which lay nestled at the foot of the mountains on the opposite shore. Troezen was not fifty miles by water from Athens, and the purple-peaked island of AEgina lay between them; but to the people of that early time the distance seemed very great, and it was not often that ships passed from one place to the other. And as for going by land round the great bend of the sea, that was a thing so fraught with danger that no man had ever dared try it.

King Pittheus of Troezen was right glad to see AEgeus, for they had been boys together, and he welcomed him to his city and did all that he could to make his visit a pleasant one. So, day after day, there was feasting and merriment and music in the marble halls of old Troezen, and the two kings spent many a happy hour in talking of the deeds of their youth and of the mighty heroes whom both had known. And when the time came for the ship to sail back to Athens, AEgeus was not ready to go. He said he would stay yet a little longer in Troezen, for that the elders of the city would manage things well at home; and so the ship returned without him.

But AEgeus tarried, not so much for the rest and enjoyment which he was having in the home of his old friend, as for the sake of AEthra, his old friend's daughter. For AEthra was as fair as a summer morning, and she was the joy and pride of Troezen; and AEgeus was never so happy as when in her presence. So it happened that some time after the ship had sailed, there was a wedding in the halls of King Pittheus; but it was kept a secret, for AEgeus feared that his nephews, if they heard of it, would be very angry and would send men to Troezen to do him harm.

Month after month passed by, and still AEgeus lingered with his bride and trusted his elders to see to the affairs of Athens. Then one morning, when the gardens of Troezen were full of roses and the heather was green on the hills, a babe was born to AEthra-a boy with a fair face and strong arms and eyes as sharp and as bright as the mountain eagle's. And now AEgeus was more loth to return home than he had been before, and he went up on the mountain which overlooks Troezen, and prayed to Athena, the queen of the air, to give him wisdom and show him what to do. Even while he prayed there came a ship into the harbor, bringing a letter to AEgeus and alarming news from Athens.

"Come home without delay"-these were words of the letter which the elders had

82

sent-"come home quickly, or Athens will be lost. A great king from beyond the sea, Minos of Crete, is on the way with ships and a host of fighting men; and he declares that he will carry sword and fire within our walls, and will slay our young men and make our children his slaves. Come and save us!"

"It is the call of duty," said AEgeus; and with a heavy heart he made ready to go at once across the sea to the help of his people. But he could not take AEthra and her babe, for fear of his lawless nephews, who would have slain them both.

"Best of wives," he said, when the hour for parting had come, "listen to me, for I shall never see your father's halls, nor dear old Troezen, nor perhaps your own fair face, again. Do you remember the old plane tree which stands on the mountain side, and the great flat stone which lies a little way beyond it, and which no man but myself has ever been able to lift? Under that stone, I have hidden my sword and the sandals which I brought from Athens. There they shall lie until our child is strong enough to lift the stone and take them for his own. Care for him, AEthra, until that time; and then, and not till then, you may tell him of his father, and bid him seek me in Athens."

Then AEgeus kissed his wife and the babe, and went on board the ship; the sailors shouted; the oars were dipped into the waves; the white sail was spread to the breeze; and AEthra from her palace window saw the vessel speed away over the blue waters towards AEgina and the distant Attic shore.

II. SWORD AND SANDALS.

Year after year went by, and yet no word reached AEthra from her husband on the other side of the sea. Often and often she would climb the mountain above Troezen, and sit there all day, looking out over the blue waters and the purple hills of AEgina to the dim, distant shore beyond. Now and then she could see a white-winged ship sailing in the offing; but men said that it was a Cretan vessel, and very likely was filled with fierce Cretan warriors, bound upon some cruel errand of war. Then it was rumored that King Minos had seized upon all the ships of Athens, and had burned a part of the city, and had forced the people to pay him a most grievous tribute. But further than this there was no news.

In the meanwhile AEthra's babe had grown to be a tall, ruddy-cheeked lad, strong as a mountain lion; and she had named him Theseus. On the day that he was fifteen years old he went with her up to the top of the mountain, and with her looked out over the sea.

"Ah, if only your father would come!" she sighed.

"My father?" said Theseus. "Who is my father, and why are you always watching

83

and waiting and wishing that he would come? Tell me about him."

And she answered: "My child, do you see the great flat stone which lies there, half buried in the ground, and covered with moss and trailing ivy? Do you think you can lift it?"

"I will try, mother," said Theseus. And he dug his fingers into the ground beside it, and grasped its uneven edges, and tugged and lifted and strained until his breath came hard and his arms ached and his body was covered with sweat; but the stone was moved not at all. At last he said, "The task is too hard for me until I have grown stronger. But why do you wish me to lift it?"

"When you are strong enough to lift it," answered AEthra, "I will tell you about your father."

After that the boy went out every day and practiced at running and leaping and throwing and lifting; and every day he rolled some stone out of its place. At first he could move only a little weight, and those who saw him laughed as he pulled and puffed and grew red in the face, but never gave up until he had lifted it. And little by little he grew stronger, and his muscles became like iron bands, and his limbs were like mighty levers for strength. Then on his next birthday he went up on the mountain with his mother, and again tried to lift the great stone. But it remained fast in its place and was not moved.

"I am not yet strong enough, mother," he said.

"Have patience, my son," said AEthra.

So he went on again with his running and leaping and throwing and lifting; and he practiced wrestling, also, and tamed the wild horses of the plain, and hunted the lions among the mountains; and his strength and swiftness and skill were the wonder of all men, and old Troezen was filled with tales of the deeds of the boy Theseus. Yet when he tried again on his seventeenth birthday, he could not move the great flat stone that lay near the plane tree on the mountain side.

"Have patience, my son," again said AEthra; but this time the tears were standing in her eyes.

So he went back again to his exercising; and he learned to wield the sword and the battle ax and to throw tremendous weights and to carry tremendous burdens. And men said that since the days of Hercules there was never so great strength in one body. Then, when he was a year older, he climbed the mountain yet another time with his mother, and he stooped and took hold of the stone, and it yielded to his touch; and, lo, when he had lifted it quite out of the ground, he found underneath it a sword of bronze and sandals of gold, and these he gave to his mother.

"Tell me now about my father," he said.

027

SHE BUCKLED THE SWORD TO HIS BELT

AEthra knew that the time had come for which she had waited so long, and she buckled the sword to his belt and fastened the sandals upon his feet. Then she told him who his father was, and why he had left them in Troezen, ands how he had said that when the lad was strong enough to lift the great stone, he must take the sword and sandals and go and seek him in Athens.

Theseus was glad when he heard this, and his proud eyes flashed with eagerness as he said: "I am ready, mother; and I will set out for Athens this very day."

Then they walked down the mountain together and told King Pittheus what had happened, and showed him the sword and the sandals. But the old man shook his head sadly and tried to dissuade Theseus from going.

"How can you go to Athens in these lawless times?" he said. "The sea is full of pirates. In fact, no ship from Troezen has sailed across the Saronic Sea since your kingly father went home to the help of his people, eighteen years ago."

Then, finding that this only made Theseus the more determined, he said: "But if you must go, I will have a new ship built for you, stanch and stout and fast sailing; and fifty of the bravest young men in Troezen shall go with you; and mayhap with fair winds and fearless hearts you shall escape the pirates and reach Athens in safety."

"Which is the most perilous way?" asked Theseus-"to go by ship or to make the journey on foot round the great bend of land?"

"The seaway is full enough of perils," said his grandfather, "but the landway is beset with dangers tenfold greater. Even if there were good roads and no hindrances, the journey round the shore is a long one and would require many days. But there are rugged mountains to climb, and wide marshes to cross, and dark forests to go through. There is hardly a footpath in all that wild region, nor any place to find rest or shelter; and the woods are full of wild beasts, and dreadful dragons lurk in the marshes, and many cruel robber giants dwell in the mountains."

"Well," said Theseus, "if there are more perils by land than by sea, then I shall go by land, and I go at once."

"But you will at least take fifty young men, your companions, with you?" said King Pittheus.

"Not one shall go with me," said Theseus; and he stood up and played with his sword hilt, and laughed at the thought of fear.

Then when there was nothing more to say, he kissed his mother and bade his grandfather good-by, and went out of Troezen towards the trackless coastland which lay to the west and north. And with blessings and tears the king and AEthra followed him to the city gates, and watched him until his tall form was lost to sight among the trees which bordered the shore of the sea.

III. ROUGH ROADS AND ROBBERS.

With a brave heart Theseus walked on, keeping the sea always upon his right. Soon the old city of Troezen was left far behind, and he came to the great marshes, where the ground sank under him at every step, and green pools of stagnant water lay on both sides of the narrow pathway. But no fiery dragon came out of the reeds to meet him; and so he walked on and on till he came to the rugged mountain land which bordered the western shore of the sea. Then he climbed one slope after another, until at last he stood on the summit of a gray peak from which he could see the whole country spread out around him. Then downward and onward he went again, but his way led him through dark mountain glens, and along the edges of mighty precipices, and underneath many a frowning cliff, until he came to a dreary wood where the trees grew tall and close together and the light of the sun was seldom seen.

In that forest there dwelt a robber giant, called Club-carrier, who was the terror of all the country. For oftentimes he would go down into the valleys where the shepherds fed their flocks, and would carry off not only sheep and lambs, but sometimes children and the men themselves. It was his custom to hide in the thickets of underbrush, close to a pathway, and, when a traveler passed that way, leap out upon him and beat him to death. When he saw Theseus coming through the woods, he thought that he would have a rich prize, for he knew from the youth's dress and manner that he must be a prince. He lay on the ground, where leaves of ivy and tall grass screened him from view, and held his great iron club ready to strike.

But Theseus had sharp eyes and quick ears, and neither beast nor robber giant could have taken him by surprise. When Club-carrier leaped out of his hiding place to strike him down, the young man dodged aside so quickly that the heavy club struck the ground behind him; and then, before the robber giant could raise it for a second stroke, Theseus seized the fellow's legs and tripped him up.

Club-carrier roared loudly, and tried to strike again; but Theseus wrenched the club out of his hands, and then dealt him such a blow on the head that he never again harmed travelers passing through the forest. Then the youth went on his way, carrying the huge club on his shoulder, and singing a song of victory, and looking sharply around him for any other foes that might be lurking among the trees.

Just over the ridge of the next mountain he met an old man who warned him not to go any farther. He said that close by a grove of pine trees, which he would soon pass on his way down the slope, there dwelt a robber named Sinis, who was very cruel to strangers.

"He is called Pine-bender," said the old man; "for when he has caught a traveler, he bends two tall, lithe pine trees to the ground and binds his captive to them-a hand and a foot to the top of one, and a hand and a foot to the top of the other. Then he lets the trees fly up, and he roars with laughter when he sees the traveler's body torn in sunder."

"It seems to me," said Theseus, "that it is full time to rid the world of such a monster;" and he thanked the kind man who had warned him, and hastened onward, whistling merrily as he went down towards the grove of pines.

Soon he came in sight of the robber's house, built near the foot of a jutting cliff. Behind it was a rocky gorge and a roaring mountain stream; and in front of it was a garden wherein grew all kinds of rare plants and beautiful flowers. But the tops of the pine trees below it were laden with the bones of unlucky travelers, which hung bleaching white in the sun and wind.

On a stone by the roadside sat Sinis himself; and when he saw Theseus coming, he ran to meet him, twirling a long rope in his hands and crying out:

"Welcome, welcome, dear prince! Welcome to our inn-the true Traveler's Rest!"

"What kind of entertainment have you?" asked Theseus. "Have you a pine tree bent down to the ground and ready for me?"

"Ay; two of them!" said the robber. "I knew that you were coming, and I bent two of them for you."

As he spoke he threw his rope towards Theseus and tried to entangle him in its coils. But the young man leaped aside, and when the robber rushed upon him, he dodged beneath his hands and seized his legs, as he had seized Club-carrier's, and threw him heavily to the ground. Then the two wrestled together among the trees, but not long, for Sinis was no match for his lithe young foe; and Theseus knelt upon the robber's back as he lay prone among the leaves, and tied him with his own cord to the two pine trees which were already bent down. "As you would have done unto me, so will I do unto you," he said.

Then Pine-bender wept and prayed and made many a fair promise; but Theseus would not hear him. He turned away, the trees sprang up, and the robber's body was left dangling from their branches.

Now this old Pine-bender had a daughter named Perigune, who was no more like him than a fair and tender violet is, like the gnarled old oak at whose feet it nestles; and it was she who cared for the flowers and the rare plants which grew in the garden by the robber's house. When she saw how Theseus had dealt with her father, she was afraid and ran to hide herself from him.

"Oh, save me, dear plants!" she cried, for she often talked to the flowers as though they could understand her. "Dear plants, save me; and I will never pluck your leaves nor harm you in any way so long as I live."

There was one of the plants which up to that time had had no leaves, but came up out of the ground looking like a mere club or stick. This plant took pity on the maiden. It began at once to send out long feathery branches with delicate green leaves, which grew so fast that Perigune was soon hidden from sight beneath them. Theseus knew that she must be somewhere in the garden, but he could not find her, so well did the feathery branches conceal her. So he called to her:

"Perigune," he said, "you need not fear me; for I know that you are gentle and good, and it is only against things dark and cruel that I lift up my hand."

The maiden peeped from her hiding-place, and when she saw the fair face of the youth and heard his kind voice, she came out, trembling, and talked with him. And Theseus rested that evening in her house, and she picked some of her choicest flowers for him and gave him food. But when in the morning the dawn began to appear in the east, and the stars grew dim above the mountain peaks, he bade her farewell and journeyed onward over the hills. And Perigune tended her plants and watched her flowers in the lone garden in the midst of the piny grove; but she never plucked the stalks of asparagus nor used them for food, and when she afterwards became the wife of a hero and had children and grandchildren and great-grandchildren, she taught them all to spare the plant which had taken pity upon her in her need.

The road which Theseus followed now led him closer to the shore, and by and by he came to a place where the mountains seemed to rise sheer out of the sea, and there was only a, narrow path high up along the side of the cliff. Far down beneath his feet he could hear the waves dashing evermore against the rocky wall, while above him the mountain eagles circled and screamed, and gray crags and barren peaks glistened in the sunlight.

But Theseus went on fearlessly and came at last to a place where a spring of clear water bubbled out from a cleft in the rock; and there the path was narrower still, and the low doorway of a cavern opened out upon it. Close by the spring sat a red-faced giant, with a huge club across his knees, guarding the road so that no one could pass; and in the sea at the foot of the cliff basked a huge turtle, its leaden eyes looking always upward for its food. Theseus knew-for Perigune had told him-that this was the dwelling-place of a robber named Sciron, who was the terror of all the coast, and whose custom it was to make strangers wash his feet, so that while they were doing so, he might kick them over the cliff to be eaten, by his pet turtle below.

When Theseus came up, the robber raised his club, and said fiercely: "No man can pass here until he has washed my feet! Come, set to work!"

Then Theseus smiled, and said: "Is your turtle hungry to-day? and do you want me to feed him?" The robber's eyes flashed fire, and he said, "You shall feed him, but you shall wash my feet first;" and with that he brandished his club in the air and rushed forward to strike.

But Theseus was ready for him. With the iron club which he had taken from Club-carrier in the forest he met the blow midway, and the robber's weapon was knocked out of his hands and sent spinning away over the edge of the cliff. Then Sciron, black with rage, tried to grapple with him; but Theseus was too quick for that. He dropped his club and seized Sciron by the throat; he pushed him back against the ledge on which he had been sitting; he threw him sprawling upon the sharp rocks, and held him there, hanging half way over the cliff.

"Enough! enough!" cried the robber. "Let me up, and you may pass on your way."

"It is not enough," said Theseus; and he drew his sword and sat down by the side of the spring. "You must wash my feet now. Come, set to work!"

Then Sciron, white with fear, washed his feet.

"And now," said Theseus, when the task was ended, "as you have done unto others, so will I do unto you."

There was a scream in mid air which the mountain eagles answered from above; there was a great splashing in the water below, and the turtle fled in terror from its lurking place. Then the sea cried out: "I will have naught to do with so vile a wretch!" and a great wave cast the body of Sciron out upon the shore. But it had no sooner touched the ground than the land cried out: "I will have naught to do with so vile a wretch!" and there was a sudden earthquake, and the body of Sciron was thrown back into the sea. Then the sea waxed furious, a raging storm arose, the waters were lashed into foam, and the waves with one mighty effort threw the detested body high into the air; and there it would have hung unto this day had not the air itself disdained to give it lodging and changed it into a huge black rock. And this rock, which men say is the body of Sciron, may still be seen, grim, ugly, and desolate; and one third of it lies in the sea, one third is embedded in the sandy shore, and one third is exposed to the air.

IV. WRESTLER AND WRONG-DOER.

Keeping the sea always in view, Theseus went onward a long day's journey to the north and east; and he left the rugged mountains behind and came down into the valleys and into a pleasant plain where there were sheep and cattle pasturing and where there were many fields of ripening grain. The fame of his deeds had gone before him, and men and women came crowding to the roadside to see the hero who had slain Club-carrier and Pine-bender and grim old Sciron of the cliff.

"Now we shall live in peace," they cried; "for the robbers who devoured our flocks and our children are no more."

Then Theseus passed through the old town of Megara, and followed the shore of the bay towards the sacred city of Eleusis.

"Do not go into Eleusis, but take the road which leads round it through the hills," whispered a poor man who was carrying a sheep to market.

"Why shall I do that?" asked Theseus.

"Listen, and I will tell you," was the answer. "There is a king in Eleusis whose name is Cercyon, and he is a great wrestler. He makes every stranger who comes into the city wrestle with him; and such is the strength of his arms that when he has overcome a man he crushes the life out of his body. Many travelers come to Eleusis, but no one ever goes away."

"But I will both come and go away," said Theseus; and with his club upon his shoulder, he strode onward into the sacred city.

"Where is Cercyon, the wrestler?" he asked of the warden at the gate.

"The king is dining in his marble palace," was the answer. "If you wish to save yourself, turn now and flee before he has heard of your coming."

"Why should I flee?" asked Theseus. "I am not afraid;" and he walked on through the narrow street to old Cercyon's palace.

The king was sitting at his table, eating and drinking; and he grinned hideously as he thought of the many noble young men whose lives he had destroyed. Theseus went up boldly to the door, and cried out:

"Cercyon, come out and wrestle with me!"

"Ah!" said the king, "here comes another young fool whose days are numbered. Fetch him in and let him dine with me; and after that he shall have his fill of wrestling."

So Theseus was given a place at the table of the king, and the two sat there and ate and stared at each other, but spoke not a word. And Cercyon, as he looked at the young man's sharp eyes and his fair face and silken hair, had half a mind to bid him go in peace and seek not to test his strength and skill. But when they had finished, Theseus arose and laid aside his sword and his sandals and his iron club, and stripped himself of his robes, and said:

"Come now, Cercyon, if you are not afraid; come, and wrestle with me."

Then the two went out into the courtyard where many a young man had met his fate, and there they wrestled until the sun went down, and neither could gain aught of advantage over the other. But it was plain that the trained skill of Theseus would, in the end, win against the brute strength of Cercyon. Then the men of Eleusis who stood watching the contest, saw the youth lift the giant king bodily into the air and hurl him headlong over his shoulder to the hard pavement beyond.

"As you have done to others, so will I do unto you!" cried Theseus.

But grim old Cercyon neither moved nor spoke; and when the youth turned his body over and looked into his cruel face, he saw that the life had quite gone out of him.

Then the people of Eleusis came to Theseus and wanted to make him their king. "You have slain the tyrant who was the bane of Eleusis," they said, "and we have heard how you have also rid the world of the giant robbers who were the terror of the land. Come now and be our king; for we know that you will rule over us wisely and well."

"Some day," said Theseus, "I will be your king, but not now; for there are other deeds for me to do." And with that he donned his sword and his sandals and his princely cloak, and threw his great iron club upon his shoulder, and went out of Eleusis; and all the people ran after him for quite a little way, shouting, "May good fortune be with you, O king, and may Athena bless and guide you!"

V. PROCRUSTES THE PITILESS.

91

Athens was now not more than twenty miles away, but the road thither led through the Parnes Mountains, and was only a narrow path winding among the rocks and up and down many a lonely wooded glen. Theseus had seen worse and far more dangerous roads than this, and so he strode bravely onward, happy in the thought that he was so near the end of his long journey. But it was very slow traveling among the mountains, and he was not always sure that he was following the right path. The sun was almost down when he came to a broad green valley where the trees had been cleared away. A little river flowed through the middle of this valley, and on either side were grassy meadows where cattle were grazing; and on a hillside close by, half hidden among the trees, there was a great stone house with vines running over its walls and roof.

While Theseus was wondering who it could be that lived in this pretty but lonely place, a man came out of the house and hurried down to the road to meet him. He was a well-dressed man, and his face was wreathed with smiles; and he bowed low to Theseus and invited him kindly to come up to the house and be his guest that night.

"This is a lonely place," he said, "and it is not often that travelers pass this way. But there is nothing that gives me so much joy as to find strangers and feast them at my table and hear them tell of the things they have seen and heard. Come up, and sup with me, and lodge under my roof; and you shall sleep on a wonderful bed which I have-a bed which fits every guest and cures him of every ill."

Theseus was pleased with the man's ways, and as he was both hungry and tired, he went up with him and sat down under the vines by the door; and the man said:

"Now I will go in and make the bed ready for you, and you can lie down upon it and rest; and later, when you feel refreshed, you shall sit at my table and sup with me, and I will listen to the pleasant tales which I know you will tell."

When he had gone into the house, Theseus looked around him to see what sort of a place it was. He was filled with surprise at the richness of it-at the gold and silver and beautiful things with which every room seemed to be adorned-for it was indeed a place fit for a prince. While he was looking and wondering, the vines before him were parted and the fair face of a young girl peeped out.

"Noble stranger," she whispered, "do not lie down on my master's bed, for those who do so never rise again. Fly down the glen and hide yourself in the deep woods ere he returns, or else there will be no escape for you."

"Who is your master, fair maiden, that I should be afraid of him?" asked Theseus.

"Men call him Procrustes, or the Stretcher," said the girl-and she talked low and fast. "He is a robber. He brings hither all the strangers that he finds traveling through the mountains. He puts them on his iron bed. He robs them of all they have. No one who comes into his house ever goes out again."

"Why do they call him the Stretcher? And what is that iron bed of his?" asked Theseus, in no wise alarmed.

"Did he not tell you that it fits all guests?" said the girl; "and most truly it does fit them. For if a traveler is too long, Procrustes hews off his legs until he is of the right length; but if he is too short, as is the case with most guests, then he stretches his limbs and body with ropes until he is long enough. It is for this reason that men call him the Stretcher."

"Methinks that I have heard of this Stretcher before," said Theseus; and then he remembered that some one at Eleusis had warned him to beware of the wily robber, Procrustes, who lurked in the glens of the Parnes peaks and lured travelers into his den.

"Hark! hark!" whispered the girl. "I hear him coming!" And the vine leaves closed over her hiding-place.

The very next moment Procrustes stood in the door, bowing and smiling as though he had never done any harm to his fellow men.

"My dear young friend," he said, "the bed is ready, and I will show you the way. After you have taken a pleasant little nap, we will sit down at table, and you may tell me of the wonderful things which you have seen in the course of your travels."

Theseus arose and followed his host; and when they had come into an inner chamber, there, surely enough, was the bedstead, of iron, very curiously wrought, and upon it a soft couch which seemed to invite him to lie down and rest. But Theseus, peering about, saw the ax and the ropes with cunning pulleys lying hidden behind the curtains; and he saw, too, that the floor was covered with stains of blood.

"Now, my dear young friend," said Procrustes, "I pray you to lie down and take your ease; for I know that you have traveled far and are faint from want of rest and sleep. Lie down, and while sweet slumber overtakes you, I will have a care that no unseemly noise, nor buzzing fly, nor vexing gnat disturbs your dreams."

"Is this your wonderful bed?" asked Theseus.

"It is," answered Procrustes, "and you need but to lie down upon it, and it will fit you perfectly."

93

"But you must lie upon it first," said Theseus, "and let me see how it will fit itself to your stature."

Ha
Ha

"Ah, no," said Procrustes, "for then the spell would be broken," and as he spoke his cheeks grew ashy pale.

"But I tell you, you must lie upon it," said Theseus; and he seized the trembling man around the waist and threw him by force upon the bed. And no sooner was he prone upon the couch than curious iron arms reached out and clasped his body in their embrace and held him down so that he could not move hand or foot. The wretched man shrieked and cried for mercy; but Theseus stood over him and looked him straight in the eye.

"Is this the kind of bed on which you have your guests lie down?" he asked.

But Procrustes answered not a word. Then Theseus brought out the ax and the ropes and the pulleys, and asked him what they were for, and why they were hidden in the chamber. He was still silent, and could do nothing now but tremble and weep.

"Is it true," said Theseus, "that you have lured hundreds of travelers into your den only to rob them? Is it true that it is your wont to fasten them in this bed, and then chop off their legs or stretch them out until they fit the iron frame? Tell me, is this true?"

"It is true! it is true!" sobbed Procrustes; "and now kindly touch the spring above my head and let me go, and you shall have everything that I possess."

But Theseus turned away. "You are caught," he said, "in the trap which you set for others and for me. There is no mercy for the man who shows no mercy;" and he went out of the room, and left the wretch to perish by his own cruel device.

Theseus looked through the house and found there great wealth of gold and silver and costly things which Procrustes had taken from the strangers who had fallen into his hands. He went into the dining hall, and there indeed was the table spread with a rich feast of meats and drinks and delicacies such as no king would scorn; but there was a seat and a plate for only the host, and none at all for guests.

Then the girl whose fair face Theseus had seen among the vines, came running into the house; and she seized the young hero's hands and blessed and thanked him because he had rid the world of the cruel Procrustes.

"Only a month ago," she said, "my father, a rich merchant of Athens, was traveling towards Eleusis, and I was with him, happy and care-free as any bird in the green woods. This robber lured us into his den, for we had much gold with us. My father, he stretched upon his iron bed; but me, he made his slave."

Then Theseus called together all the inmates of the house, poor wretches whom Procrustes had forced to serve him; and he parted the robber's spoils among them and told them that they were free to go wheresoever they wished. And on the next day he went on, through the narrow crooked ways among the mountains and hills, and came at last to the plain of Athens, and saw the noble city and, in its midst, the rocky height where the great Temple of Athena stood; and, a little way from the temple, he saw the white walls of the palace of the king.

When Theseus entered the city and went walking up the street everybody wondered who the tall, fair youth could be. But the fame of his deeds had gone before him, and soon it was whispered that this was the hero who had slain the robbers in the mountains and had wrestled with Cercyon at Eleusis and had caught Procrustes in his own cunning trap.

"Tell us no such thing!" said some butchers who were driving their loaded carts to market. "The lad is better suited to sing sweet songs to the ladies than to fight robbers and wrestle with giants."

"See his silken black hair!" said one.

"And his girlish face!" said another.

"And his long coat dangling about his legs!" said a third.

"And his golden sandals!" said a fourth.

Don't judge a book by its cover

"Ha! ha!" laughed the first; "I wager that he never lifted a ten-pound weight in his life. Think of such a fellow as he hurling old Sciron from the cliffs! Nonsense!"

Theseus heard all this talk as he strode along, and it angered him not a little; but he had not come to Athens to quarrel with butchers. Without speaking a word he walked straight up to the foremost cart, and, before its driver had time to think, took hold of the slaughtered ox that was being hauled to market, and hurled it high over the tops of the houses into the garden beyond. Then he did likewise with the oxen in the second, the third, and the fourth wagons, and, turning about, went on his way, and left the wonder-stricken butchers staring after him, speechless, in the street.

He climbed the stairway which led to the top of the steep, rocky hill, and his heart beat fast in his bosom as he stood on the threshold of his father's palace.

"Where is the king?" he asked of the guard.

95

"You cannot see the king," was the answer; "but I will take you to his nephews."

The man led the way into the feast hall, and there Theseus saw his fifty cousins sitting about the table, and eating and drinking and making merry; and there was a great noise of revelry in the hall, the minstrels singing and playing, and the slave girls dancing, and the half-drunken princes shouting and cursing. As Theseus stood in the doorway, knitting his eyebrows and clinching his teeth for the anger which he felt, one of the feasters saw him, and cried out:

"See the tall fellow in the doorway! What does he want here?"

028

'GREAT KING,' HE SAID, 'I AM A STRANGER IN ATHENS.'

"Yes, girl-faced stranger," said another, "what do you want here?"

"I am here," said Theseus, "to ask that hospitality which men of our race never refuse to give."

"Nor do we refuse," cried they. "Come in, and eat and drink and be our guest."

"I will come in," said Theseus, "but I will be the guest of the king. Where is he?"

"Never mind the king," said one of his cousins. "He is taking his ease, and we reign in his stead."

But Theseus strode boldly through the feast hall and went about the palace asking for the king. At last he found AEgeus, lonely and sorrowful, sitting in an inner chamber. The heart of Theseus was very sad as he saw the lines of care upon the old man's face, and marked his trembling, halting ways.

"Great king," he said, "I am a stranger in Athens, and I have come to you to ask food and shelter and friendship such as I know you never deny to those of noble rank and of your own race."

"And who are you, young man?" said the king.

"I am Theseus," was the answer.

"What? the Theseus who has rid the world of the mountain robbers, and of Cercyon the wrestler, and of Procrustes, the pitiless Stretcher?"

"I am he," said Theseus; "and I come from old Troezen, on the other side of the

Saronic Sea."

The king started and turned very pale.

"Troezen! Troezen!" he cried. Then checking himself, he said, "Yes! yes! You are welcome, brave stranger, to such shelter and food and friendship as the King of Athens can give."

Now it so happened that there was with the king a fair but wicked witch named Medea, who had so much power over him that he never dared to do anything without asking her leave. So he turned to her, and said: "Am I not right, Medea, in bidding this young hero welcome?"

"You are right, King AEgeus," she said; "and let him be shown at once to your guest chamber, that he may rest himself and afterwards dine with us at your own table."

Medea had learned by her magic arts who Theseus was, and she was not at all pleased to have him in Athens; for she feared that when he should make himself known to the king, her own power would be at an end. So, while Theseus was resting himself in the guest chamber, she told AEgeus that the young stranger was no hero at all, but a man whom his nephews had hired to kill him, for they had grown tired of waiting for him to die. The poor old king was filled with fear, for he believed her words; and he asked her what he should do to save his life.

"Let me manage it," she said. "The young man will soon come down to dine with us. I will drop poison into a glass of wine, and at the end of the meal I will give it to him. Nothing can be easier."

So, when the hour came, Theseus sat down to dine with the king and Medea; and while he ate he told of his deeds and of how he had overcome the robber giants, and Cercyon the wrestler, and Procrustes the pitiless; and as the king listened, his heart yearned strangely towards the young man, and he longed to save him from Medea's poisoned cup. Then Theseus paused in his talk to help himself to a piece of the roasted meat, and, as was the custom of the time, drew his sword to carve it- for you must remember that all these things happened long ago, before people had learned to use knives and forks at the table. As the sword flashed from its scabbard, AEgeus saw the letters that were engraved upon it-the initials of his own name. He knew at once that it was the sword which he had hidden so many years before under the stone on the mountain side above Troezen.

"My son! my son!" he cried; and he sprang up and dashed the cup of poisoned wine from the table, and flung his arms around Theseus. It was indeed a glad meeting for both father and son, and they had many things to ask and to tell. As for the wicked Medea, she knew that her day of rule was past. She ran out of the

97

palace, and whistled a loud, shrill call; and men say that a chariot drawn by dragons came rushing through the air, and that she leaped into it and was carried away, and no one ever saw her again.

The very next morning, AEgeus sent out his heralds, to make it known through all the city that Theseus was his son, and that he would in time be king in his stead. When the fifty nephews heard this, they were angry and alarmed.

"Shall this upstart cheat us out of our heritage?" they cried; and they made a plot to waylay and kill Theseus in a grove close by the city gate.

Right cunningly did the wicked fellows lay their trap to catch the young hero; and one morning, as he was passing that way alone, several of them fell suddenly upon him, with swords and lances, and tried to slay him outright. They were thirty to one, but he faced them boldly and held them at bay, while he shouted for help. The men of Athens, who had borne so many wrongs from the hands of the nephews, came running out from the streets; and in the fight which followed, every one of the plotters, who had lain in ambush was slain; and the other nephews, when they heard about it, fled from the city in haste and never came back again.

029

THE WONDERFUL ARTISAN.

I. PERDIX.

While Athens was still only a small city there lived within its walls a man named Daedalus who was the most skillful worker in wood and stone and metal that had ever been known. It was he who taught the people how to build better houses and how to hang their doors on hinges and how to support the roofs with pillars and posts. He was the first to fasten things together with glue; he invented the plumb-line and the auger; and he showed seamen how to put up masts in their ships and how to rig the sails to them with ropes. He built a stone palace for AEgeus, the young king of Athens, and beautified the Temple of Athena which stood on the great rocky hill in the middle of the city.

Daedalus had a nephew named Perdix whom he had taken when a boy to teach the trade of builder. But Perdix was a very apt learner, and soon surpassed his master in the knowledge of many things. His eyes were ever open to see what was going on about him, and he learned the lore of the fields and the woods. Walking one day by the sea, he picked up the backbone of a great fish, and from it he invented the saw. Seeing how a certain bird carved holes in the trunks of trees, he learned how to make and use the chisel. Then he invented the wheel which potters use in molding clay; and he made of a forked stick the first pair of compasses for

98

drawing circles; and he studied out many other curious and useful things.

Daedalus was not pleased when he saw that the lad was so apt and wise, so ready to learn, and so eager to do.

"If he keeps on in this way," he murmured, "he will be a greater man than I; his name will be remembered, and mine will be forgotten."

Day after day, while at his work, Daedalus pondered over this matter, and soon his heart was filled with hatred towards young Perdix. One morning when the two were putting up an ornament on the outer wall of Athena's temple, Daedalus bade his nephew go out on a narrow scaffold which hung high over the edge of the rocky cliff whereon the temple stood. Then, when the lad obeyed, it was easy enough, with a blow of a hammer, to knock the scaffold from its fastenings.

Poor Perdix fell headlong through the air, and he would have been dashed in pieces upon the stones at the foot of the cliff had not kind Athena seen him and taken pity upon him. While he was yet whirling through mid-air she changed him into a partridge, and he flitted away to the hills to live forever in the woods and fields which he loved so well. And to this day, when summer breezes blow and the wild flowers bloom in meadow and glade, the voice of Perdix may still sometimes be heard, calling to his mate from among the grass and reeds or amid the leafy underwoods.

II. MINOS.

As for Daedalus, when the people of Athens heard of his dastardly deed, they were filled with grief and rage-grief for young Perdix, whom all had learned to love; rage towards the wicked uncle, who loved only himself. At first they were for punishing Daedalus with the death which he so richly deserved, but when they remembered what he had done to make their homes pleasanter and their lives easier, they allowed him to live; and yet they drove him out of Athens and bade him never return.

There was a ship in the harbor just ready to start on a voyage across the sea, and in it Daedalus embarked with all his precious tools and his young son Icarus. Day after day the little vessel sailed slowly southward, keeping the shore of the mainland always upon the right. It passed Troezen and the rocky coast of Argos, and then struck boldly out across the sea.

At last the famous Island of Crete was reached, and there Daedalus landed and made himself known; and the King of Crete, who had already heard of his wondrous skill, welcomed him to his kingdom, and gave him a home in his palace, and promised that he should be rewarded with great riches and honor if he would but stay and practice his craft there as he had done in Athens.

Now the name of the King of Crete was Minos. His grandfather, whose name was also Minos, was the son of Europa, a young princess whom a white bull, it was said, had brought on his back across the sea from distant Asia. This elder Minos had been accounted the wisest of men-so wise, indeed, that Jupiter chose him to be one of the judges of the Lower World. The younger Minos was almost as wise as his grandfather; and he was brave and far-seeing and skilled as a ruler of men. He had made all the islands subject to his kingdom, and his ships sailed into every part of the world and brought back to Crete the riches of foreign lands. So it was not hard for him to persuade Daedalus to make his home with him and be the chief of his artisans.

And Daedalus built for King Minos a most wonderful palace with floors of marble and pillars of granite; and in the palace he set up golden statues which had tongues and could talk; and for splendor and beauty there was no other building in all the wide earth that could be compared with it.

There lived in those days among the hills of Crete a terrible monster called the Minotaur, the like of which has never been seen from that time until now. This creature, it was said, had the body of a man, but the face and head of a wild bull and the fierce nature of a mountain lion. The people of Crete would not have killed him if they could; for they thought that the Mighty Folk who lived with Jupiter on the mountain top had sent him among them, and that these beings would be angry if any one should take his life. He was the pest and terror of all the land. Where he was least expected, there he was sure to be; and almost every day some man, woman, or child was caught and devoured by him.

"You have done so many wonderful things," said the king to Daedalus, "can you not do something to rid the land of this Minotaur?"

"Shall I kill him?" asked Daedalus.

"Ah, no!" said the king. "That would only bring greater misfortunes upon us."

"I will build a house for him then," said Daedalus, "and you can keep him in it as a prisoner."

"But he may pine away and die if he is penned up in prison," said the king.

"He shall have plenty of room to roam about," said Daedalus; "and if you will only now and then feed one of your enemies to him, I promise you that he shall live and thrive."

So the wonderful artisan brought together his workmen, and they built a marvelous house with so many rooms in it and so many winding ways that no one who went far into it could ever find his way out again; and Daedalus called it the Labyrinth, and cunningly persuaded the Minotaur to go inside of it. The monster soon lost his way among the winding passages, but the sound of his terrible bellowings could be heard day and night as he wandered back and forth vainly trying to find some place to escape.

III. ICARUS.

Not long after this it happened that Daedalus was guilty of a deed which angered the king very greatly; and had not Minos wished him to build other buildings for him, he would have put him to death and no doubt have served him right.

"Hitherto," said the king, "I have honored you for your skill and rewarded you for your labor. But now you shall be my slave and shall serve me without hire and without any word of praise."

Then he gave orders to the guards at the city gates that they should not let Daedalus pass out at any time, and he set soldiers to watch the ships that were in port so that he could not escape by sea. But although the wonderful artisan was thus held as a prisoner, he did not build any more buildings for King Minos; he spent his time in planning how he might regain his freedom.

"All my inventions," he said to his son Icarus, "have hitherto been made to please other people; now I will invent something to please myself."

So, all through the day he pretended to be planning some great work for the king, but every night he locked himself up in his chamber and wrought secretly by candle light. By and by he had made for himself a pair of strong wings, and for Icarus another pair of smaller ones; and then, one midnight, when everybody was asleep, the two went out to see if they could fly. They fastened the wings to their shoulders with wax, and then sprang up into the air. They could not fly very far at first, but they did so well that they felt sure of doing much better in time.

The next night Daedalus made some changes in the wings. He put on an extra strap or two; he took out a feather from one wing, and put a new feather into another; and then he and Icarus went out in the moonlight to try them again. They did finely this time. They flew up to the top of the king's palace, and then they sailed away over the walls of the city and alighted on the top of a hill. But they were not ready to undertake a long journey yet; and so, just before daybreak, they flew back home. Every fair night after that they practiced with their wings, and at the end of a month they felt as safe in the air as on the ground, and could skim over the hilltops like birds.

Early one morning; before King Minos had risen from his bed, they fastened on their wings, sprang into the air, and flew out of the city. Once fairly away from the island, they turned towards the west, for Daedalus had heard of an island named Sicily, which lay hundreds of miles away, and he had made up his mind to seek a new home there.

030

HE FELT HIMSELF SINKING THROUGH THE AIR

All went well for a time, and the two bold flyers sped swiftly over the sea, skimming along only a little above the waves, and helped on their way by the brisk east wind. Towards noon the sun shone very warm, and Daedalus called out to the boy who was a little behind and told him to keep his wings cool and not fly too high. But the boy was proud of his skill in flying, and as he looked up at the sun he thought how nice it would be to soar like it high above the clouds in the blue depths of the sky.

"At any rate," said he to himself, "I will go up a little higher. Perhaps I can see the horses which draw the sun car, and perhaps I shall catch sight of their driver, the mighty sun master himself."

So he flew up higher and higher, but his father who was in front did not see him. Pretty soon, however, the heat of the sun began to melt the wax with which the boy's wings were fastened. He felt himself sinking through the air; the wings had become loosened from his shoulders. He screamed to his father, but it was too late. Daedalus turned just in time to see Icarus fall headlong into the waves. The water was very deep there, and the skill of the wonderful artisan could not save his child. He could only look with sorrowing eyes at the unpitying sea, and fly on alone to distant Sicily. There, men say, he lived for many years, but he never did any great work, nor built anything half so marvelous as the Labyrinth of Crete. And the sea in which poor Icarus was drowned was called forever afterward by his name, the Icarian Sea.

031

THE CRUEL TRIBUTE.

I. THE TREATY.

Minos, king of Crete, had made war upon Athens. He had come with a great fleet of ships and an army, and had burned the merchant vessels in the harbor, and had overrun all the country and the coast even to Megara, which lies to the west. He had laid waste the fields and gardens round about Athens, had pitched his camp

102

close to the walls, and had sent word to the Athenian rulers that on the morrow he would march into their city with fire and sword and would slay all their young men and would pull down all their houses, even to the Temple of Athena, which stood on the great hill above the town. Then AEgeus, the king of Athens, with the twelve elders who were his helpers, went out to see King Minos and to treat with him.

"O mighty king," they said, "what have we done that you should wish thus to destroy us from the earth?"

"O cowardly and shameless men," answered King Minos, "why do you ask this foolish question, since you can but know the cause of my wrath? I had an only son, Androgeos by name, and he was dearer to me than the hundred cities of Crete and the thousand islands of the sea over which I rule. Three years ago he came hither to take part in the games which you held in honor of Athena, whose temple you have built on yonder hilltop. You know how he overcame all your young men in the sports, and how your people honored him with song and dance and laurel crown. But when your king, this same AEgeus who stands before me now, saw how everybody ran after him and praised his valor, he was filled with envy and laid plans to kill him. Whether he caused armed men to waylay him on the road to Thebes, or whether as some say he sent him against a certain wild bull of your country to be slain by that beast, I know not; but you cannot deny that the young man's life was taken from him through the plotting of this AEgeus."

"But we do deny it-we do deny it!" cried the elders. "For at that very time our king was sojourning at Troezen on the other side of the Saronic Sea, and he knew nothing of the young prince's death. We ourselves managed the city's affairs while he was abroad, and we know whereof we speak. Androgeos was slain, not through the king's orders but by the king's nephews, who hoped to rouse your anger against AEgeus so that you would drive him from Athens and leave the kingdom to one of them."

"Will you swear that what you tell me is true?" said Minos.

"We will swear it," they said.

"Now then," said Minos, "you shall hear my decree. Athens has robbed me of my dearest treasure, a treasure that can never be restored to me; so, in return, I require from Athens, as tribute, that possession which is the dearest and most precious to her people; and it shall be destroyed cruelly as my son was destroyed."

"The condition is hard," said the elders, "but it is just. What is the tribute which you require?"

"Has the king a son?" asked Minos.

The face of King AEgeus lost all its color and he trembled as he thought of a little child then with its mother at Troezen, on the other side of the Saronic Sea. But the elders knew nothing about that child, and they answered:

"Alas, no! he has no son; but he has fifty nephews who are eating up his substance and longing for the time to come when one of them shall be king; and, as we have said, it was they who slew the young prince, Androgeos."

"I have naught to do with those fellows," said Minos; "you may deal with them as you like. But you ask what is the tribute that I require, and I will tell you. Every year when the springtime comes and the roses begin to bloom, you shall choose seven of your noblest youths and seven of your fairest maidens, and shall send them to me in a ship which your king shall provide. This is the tribute which you shall pay to me, Minos, king of Crete; and if you fail for a single time, or delay even a day, my soldiers shall tear down your walls and burn your city and put your men to the sword and sell your wives and children as slaves."

"We agree to all this, O King," said the elders; "for it is the least of two evils. But tell us now, what shall be the fate of the seven youths and the seven maidens?"

"In Crete," answered Minos, "there is a house called the Labyrinth, the like of which you have never seen. In it there are a thousand chambers and winding ways, and whosoever goes even a little way into them can never find his way out again. Into this house the seven youths and the seven maidens shall be thrust, and they shall be left there-"

"To perish with hunger?" cried the elders.

"To be devoured by a monster whom men call the Minotaur," said Minos.

Then King AEgeus and the elders covered their faces and wept and went slowly back into the city to tell their people of the sad and terrible conditions upon which Athens could alone be saved.

"It is better that a few should perish than that the whole city should be destroyed," they said.

II. THE TRIBUTE.

Years passed by. Every spring when the roses began to bloom seven youths and seven maidens were put on board of a black-sailed ship and sent to Crete to pay the tribute which King Minos required. In every house in Athens there was sorrow and dread, and the people lifted up their hands to Athena on the hilltop and cried

104

out, "How long, O Queen of the Air, how long shall this thing be?"

In the meanwhile the little child at Troezen on the other side of the sea had grown to be a man. His name, Theseus, was in everybody's mouth, for he had done great deeds of daring; and at last he had come to Athens to find his father, King AEgeus, who had never heard whether he was alive or dead; and when the youth had made himself known, the king had welcomed him to his home and all the people were glad because so noble a prince had come to dwell among them and, in time, to rule over their city.

The springtime came again. The black-sailed ship was rigged for another voyage. The rude Cretan soldiers paraded the streets; and the herald of King Minos stood at the gates and shouted:

"Yet three days, O Athenians, and your tribute will be due and must be paid!"

Then in every street the doors of the houses were shut and no man went in or out, but every one sat silent with pale cheeks, and wondered whose lot it would be to be chosen this year. But the young prince, Theseus, did not understand; for he had not been told about the tribute.

"What is the meaning of all this?" he cried. "What right has a Cretan to demand tribute in Athens? and what is this tribute of which he speaks?"

Then AEgeus led him aside and with tears told him of the sad war with King Minos, and of the dreadful terms of peace. "Now, say no more," sobbed AEgeus, "it is better that a few should die even thus than that all should be destroyed."

"But I will say more," cried Theseus. "Athens shall not pay tribute to Crete. I myself will go with these youths and maidens, and I will slay the monster Minotaur, and defy King Minos himself upon his throne."

"Oh, do not be so rash!" said the king; "for no one who is thrust into the den of the Minotaur ever comes out again. Remember that you are the hope of Athens, and do not take this great risk upon yourself."

"Say you that I am the hope of Athens?" said Theseus. "Then how can I do otherwise than go?" And he began at once to make himself ready.

On the third day all the youths and maidens of the city were brought together in the market place, so that lots might be cast for those who were to be taken. Then two vessels of brass were brought and set before King AEgeus and the herald who had come from Crete. Into one vessel they placed as many balls as there were noble youths in the city, and into the other as many as there were maidens; and all the balls were white save only seven in each vessel, and those were black as

105

ebony.

Then every maiden, without looking, reached her hand into one of the vessels and drew forth a ball, and those who took the black balls were borne away to the black ship, which lay in waiting by the shore. The young men also drew lots in like manner, but when six black balls had been drawn Theseus came quickly forward and said:

"Hold! Let no more balls be drawn. I will be the seventh youth to pay this tribute. Now let us go aboard the black ship and be off."

Then the people, and King AEgeus himself, went down to the shore to take leave of the young men and maidens, whom they had no hope of seeing again; and all but Theseus wept and were brokenhearted.

"I will come again, father," he said.

"I will hope that you may," said the old king. "If when this ship returns, I see a white sail spread above the black one, then I shall know that you are alive and well; but if I see only the black one, it will tell me that you have perished."

And now the vessel was loosed from its moorings, the north wind filled the sail, and the seven youths and seven maidens were borne away over the sea, towards the dreadful death which awaited them in far distant Crete.

III. THE PRINCESS.

At last the black ship reached the end of its voyage. The young people were set ashore, and a party of soldiers led them through the streets towards the prison, where they were to stay until the morrow. They did not weep nor cry out now, for they had outgrown their fears. But with paler faces and firm-set lips, they walked between the rows of Cretan houses, and looked neither to the right nor to the left. The windows and doors were full of people who were eager to see them.

"What a pity that such brave young men should be food for the Minotaur," said some.

"Ah, that maidens so beautiful should meet a fate so sad!" said others.

And now they passed close by the palace gate, and in it stood King Minos himself, and his daughter Ariadne, the fairest of the women of Crete.

"Indeed, those are noble young fellows!" said the king.

106

"Yes, too noble to feed the vile Minotaur," said Ariadne.

"The nobler, the better," said the king; "and yet none of them can compare with your lost brother Androgeos."

Ariadne said no more; and yet she thought that she had never seen any one who looked so much like a hero as young Theseus. How tall he was, and how handsome! How proud his eye, and how firm his step! Surely there had never been his like in Crete.

All through that night Ariadne lay awake and thought of the matchless hero, and grieved that he should be doomed to perish; and then she began to lay plans for setting him free. At the earliest peep of day she arose, and while everybody else was asleep, she ran out of the palace and hurried to the prison. As she was the king's daughter, the jailer opened the door at her bidding and allowed her to go in. There sat the seven youths and the seven maidens on the ground, but they had not lost hope. She took Theseus aside and whispered to him. She told him of a plan which she had made to save him; and Theseus promised her that, when he had slain the Minotaur, he would carry her away with him to Athens where she should live with him always. Then she gave him a sharp sword, and hid it underneath his cloak, telling him that with it alone could he hope to slay the Minotaur.

"And here is a ball of silken thread," she said. "As soon as you go into the Labyrinth where the monster is kept, fasten one end of the thread to the stone doorpost, and then unwind it as you go along. When you have slain the Minotaur, you have only to follow the thread and it will lead you back to the door. In the meanwhile I will see that your ship, is ready to sail, and then I will wait for you at the door of the Labyrinth."

032

THE JAILER OPENED THE DOOR AT HER BIDDING

Theseus thanked the beautiful princess and promised her again that if he should live to go back to Athens she should go with him and be his wife. Then with a prayer to Athena, Ariadne hastened away.

IV. THE LABYRINTH.

As soon as the sun was up the guards came to lead the young prisoners to the Labyrinth. They did not see the sword which Theseus had under his cloak, nor the tiny ball of silk which he held in his closed hand. They led the youths and maidens a long way into the Labyrinth, turning here and there, back and forth, a thousand different times, until it seemed certain that they could never find their way out again. Then the guards, by a secret passage which they alone knew, went out and left them, as they had left many others before, to wander about until they should be found by the terrible Minotaur.

"Stay close by me," said Theseus to his companions, "and with the help of Athena who dwells in her temple home in our own fair city, I will save you."

Then he drew his sword and stood in the narrow way before them; and they all lifted up their hands and prayed to Athena.

For hours they stood there, hearing no sound, and seeing nothing but the smooth, high walls on either side of the passage and the calm blue sky so high above them. Then the maidens sat down upon the ground and covered their faces and sobbed, and said:

"Oh, that he would come and put an end to our misery and our lives."

At last, late in the day, they heard a bellowing, low and faint as though far away. They listened and soon heard it again, a little louder and very fierce and dreadful.

"It is he! it is he!" cried Theseus; "and now for the fight!"

Then he shouted, so loudly that the walls of the Labyrinth answered back, and the sound was carried upward to the sky and outward to the rocks and cliffs of the mountains. The Minotaur heard him, and his bellowings grew louder and fiercer every moment.

"He is coming!" cried Theseus, and he ran forward to meet the beast. The seven maidens shrieked, but tried to stand up bravely and face their fate; and the six young men stood together with firm-set teeth and clinched fists, ready to fight to the last.

Soon the Minotaur came into view, rushing down the passage towards Theseus, and roaring most terribly. He was twice as tall as a man, and his head was like that of a bull with huge sharp horns and fiery eyes and a mouth as large as a lion's; but the young men could not see the lower part of his body for the cloud of dust which he raised in running. When he saw Theseus with the sword in his hand coming to meet him, he paused, for no one had ever faced him in that way before. Then he put his head down, and rushed forward, bellowing. But Theseus leaped quickly aside, and made a sharp thrust with his sword as he passed, and hewed off one of the monster's legs above the knee.

The Minotaur fell upon the ground, roaring and groaning and beating wildly about with his horned head and his hoof-like fists; but Theseus nimbly ran up to him and thrust the sword into his heart, and was away again before the beast could harm him. A great stream of blood gushed from the wound, and soon the Minotaur turned his face towards the sky and was dead.

Then the youths and maidens ran to Theseus and kissed his hands and feet, and thanked him for his great deed; and, as it was already growing dark, Theseus bade them follow him while he wound up the silken thread which was to lead them out of the Labyrinth. Through a thousand rooms and courts and winding ways they went, and at midnight they came to the outer door and saw the city lying in the moonlight before them; and, only a little way off, was the seashore where the black ship was moored which had brought them to Crete. The door was wide open, and beside it stood Ariadne waiting for them.

"The wind is fair, the sea is smooth, and the sailors are ready," she whispered; and she took the arm of Theseus, and all went together through the silent streets to the ship.

When the morning dawned they were far out to sea, and, looking back from the deck of the little vessel, only the white tops of the Cretan mountains were in sight.

Minos, when he arose from sleep, did not know that the youths and maidens had gotten safe out of the Labyrinth. But when Ariadne could not be found, he thought that robbers had carried her away. He sent soldiers out to search for her among the hills and mountains, never dreaming that she was now well on the way towards distant Athens.

Many days passed, and at last the searchers returned and said that the princess could nowhere be found. Then the king covered his head and wept, and said:

"Now, indeed, I am bereft of all my treasures!"

In the meanwhile, King AEgeus of Athens had sat day after day on a rock by the shore, looking and watching if by chance he might see a ship coming from the south. At last the vessel with Theseus and his companions hove in sight, but it still carried only the black sail, for in their joy the young men had forgotten to raise the white one.

"Alas! alas! my son has perished!" moaned AEgeus; and he fainted and fell forward into the sea and was drowned. And that sea, from then until now, has been called by his name, the Aegean Sea.

Thus Theseus became king of Athens.

Disclaimer and Terms of Use: The Author and Publisher have strived to be as accurate and complete as possible in the creation of this book, notwithstanding the fact that he does not warrant or represent at any time that the contents within are accurate due to the rapidly changing nature of the Internet. While all attempts have been made to verify information provided in this publication, the Author and Publisher assume no responsibility for errors, omissions, or contrary interpretation of the subject matter herein. Any perceived slights of specific persons, people, or organizations are unintentional. In practical advice books, like anything else in life, there are no guarantees of results. Readers are cautioned to rely on their own judgment about their individual circumstances and act accordingly. This book is not intended for use as a source of legal, medical, business, accounting or financial advice. All readers are advised to seek the services of competent professionals in the legal, medical, business, accounting, and finance fields.